5 Things I Know A

1. I HAVE to work really, really hard if I'm going to be Lily.
2. Landon has to be fantabsome if he is going to beat Jasper.
3. I'm not sure why I felt so weird around Jasper today.
4. I want Landon to beat Jasper—which means . . .
5. I am the worst friend in the world! ☹

Mackenzie Blue

BOOK TWO
The Secret Crush

By Tina Wells

Illustrations by Michael Segawa

HARPER
An Imprint of HarperCollinsPublishers

Library of Congress Cataloging-in-Publication Data
Wells, Tina.
    The secret crush / by Tina Wells ; illustrations by Michael Segawa. — 1st
ed.
        p.   cm. — (Mackenzie Blue ; bk.2)
    Summary: The continuing adventures of seventh-grader Mackenzie Blue as
she tries to juggle her time and attention between a developing crush, the school
musical, her family and her friends.
    ISBN 978-0-06-158313-1 (pbk.)
    [1. Middle schools—Fiction. 2. Interpersonal relations—Fiction.
3.   Friendship—Fiction.   4.   Musicals—Fiction.   5.   Diaries—Fiction.
6. Schools—Fiction.]   I. Segawa, Michael, ill.   II. Title.
PZ7.W46846Sec 2010   2009011609
[Fic]—dc22   CIP
                                                                         AC

Typography by Alison Klapthor

    12   13   14   15   16   LP/BR   10 9 8 7 6 5 4 3 2 1
                                    ❖
                      First paperback edition, 2013

For Dr. Courtney Carter, who taught me how to write a
"darn good sentence"

Marcus

Adam

Jen

Kathi

Zee

Conrad

Mackenzie Blue and the Cast

Mr. P

Missy

Landon   Chloe   Jasper

Ally

1

Cool Beans

"Anyone else?" Mr. P—short for Mr. Papademetriou—looked at the seventh graders in his instrumental music class. He held a black dry-erase marker, ready to write on the whiteboard at the front of the classroom. The students sat silent. "Come on. We're brainstorming names for our band. There's no such thing as a bad idea."

Landon Beck flicked his head to move the sun-bleached bangs that hung slightly over his eyes. "How about Seven Up?" he suggested. "You know, 'cause there are seven members of the group."

That's an amazing idea! Mackenzie Blue Carmichael thought. Of course, Landon was so cute, everything he said sounded great.

"Good one!" Kathi Barney cheered from the seat in front of Zee. Kathi's positive reaction didn't surprise Zee. She and Landon used to be a couple in sixth grade. Most of the time, Kathi acted like they still were.

"Seventh-Grade Singers?" Jen Calverez, Kathi's best friend, chimed in.

"The Brookdale Best!" Marcus Montgomery said.

Mr. P wrote quickly, putting each suggestion on his list under the ones that were already there—the Firecrackers, Cinnamon Toast, and Time Zone.

Zee adjusted the headband that she'd put into her red bob that morning. She had decorated it with tiny pink-and-purple plastic rhinestones from the craft shop. "How about the Zippers?" Zee suggested.

Kathi groaned as Mr. P wrote Zee's band name suggestion on the board. "Why? So it can be like Zee and the Zippers?" she asked. "No way!"

Zee shrugged. "I just think it sounds cool."

"It's brilliant!" Jasper Chapman defended Zee. Jasper had moved to Brookdale from London over the summer, and he was one of Zee's best friends.

"Thanks," Zee mouthed, giving Jasper a thumbs-up. He smiled.

"Keep 'em coming. There are some really cool ideas

here, guys," Mr. P said.

"Total Eclipse!" Zee's other best friend, Chloe Lawrence-Johnson, another Brookdale newbie, called out in her southern accent.

Slumping forward a little, Kathi let out a bored sigh. Chloe turned to her and stared with expectant eyes. "Everything all right, Kathi?"

Kathi just brushed her shiny, long brown hair off her shoulder. "Of course," she said, without turning around.

"Zodiac!" Landon added.

Yay! Zee silently cheered.

But there was another groan, and this time it came from the seat beside Zee. *Jasper?* Zee wondered. *What's up with that?* Jasper turned and gave her another smile.

"How about the Beans?" Kathi suggested.

"That's awesome!" Jen said. Usually, she said *everything* Kathi did was awesome—just to make her happy. But this time Zee agreed. The whole class started buzzing.

"Should we vote?" Mr. P broke in. "Who likes the Beans?"

Everyone's hand went up.

"It's unanimous!" Mr. P said as he erased the list on the board. "You are officially the Beans." The class cheered. "Nice work, Kathi," their teacher continued. "There are people who have been in the music business for decades who couldn't have come up with such a good name."

Kathi looked down as if she was embarrassed by all of the attention and doodled in the spiral notebook propped on the desk in front of her.

Chloe nudged Zee with her elbow, then pointed to Kathi. Zee stretched to look over Kathi's shoulder to read what she'd written—*Kathi Barney and the Beans*. Zee rolled her eyes at Chloe, and Chloe held back a giggle.

"So how are we going to introduce the band?" Mr. P continued.

Marcus's eyes lit up behind his black plastic glasses. "Hi,

we're the Beans?" he joked.

Mr. P smiled. "That's a good start. Then what? We're going to be more than just another school band, right? We rock!"

"We could do a concert," Jen said. "Kathi could be the lead singer."

"That's an idea," Mr. P said. "But don't you want to do something bigger?"

"How 'bout if we plan a dance for the whole school?" Chloe suggested.

Kathi pivoted in her seat to face Chloe. "You mean like a hoedown?" she asked.

"Uh, *no*. I've never been to a hoedown," Chloe said coolly. "But if you want to plan one, that's fine with me."

Mr. P nodded. "A dance *is* a fantastic idea, but I'm not sure it would show off all of your talents."

"We could do a musical," Kathi said.

Wow! Has Kathi actually come up with two great ideas? Zee thought. "Yeah—a rock-and-roll musical," she blurted out.

"Awesome!" Kathi said. Zee and Kathi looked at each other and froze. They couldn't believe that they liked each other's ideas.

"Freaky," Chloe whispered.

"Brilliant!" Jasper added.

"We could write it ourselves," Marcus said.

"*That's* what I'm talking about!" Mr. P agreed. "Everyone in favor of the Beans putting on a rock-and-roll musical, raise your hand."

Once again, all hands went up.

"Ooooh, I can't wait!" Kathi said, clapping her hands together. "It will be so much fun to be the star!"

When Zee got home from school that afternoon, she immediately changed out of her uniform and into her new favorite T-shirt and her perfect-shade-of-pink ruffle skirt. Then, sitting among the piles of clothes she *didn't* put on, she began to write in her diary.

Hi, Diary,

   I don't know how I survived without you today. So many totally exciting things happened with the band—the Beans. I left you at home because I was scared about losing you—or having someone (Kathi!) take you again and blab all my secret thoughts to the world. Like she did the first day of school. But if there was one thing that whole horrible event taught me, it's that I cannot live without you. SO I've decided to lock you up, take you to school with me from now on, and never, ever, EVER let you out of my sight. That way when I need to write down my thoughts, I can. Like NOW!

Words That Describe My Life

1. Fabulous!

2. Fantastic!

3. Awesome!

Zee stopped writing and tickled her cheek with the white feather she'd glued to the top of her pen. *Hmmm*, she thought, rereading her words. Nope. None of them described how great she felt. *That* word had not been invented yet.

4. Fantabsome!

"Fantabsome," Zee said out loud. "It shouldn't take long before everyone's saying it!" Satisfied, she closed her diary and locked it. Then she slipped the braided red cord that held the key around her neck. "If I ever lose my diary again—which I won't," Zee told herself, "it's going to be impossible for anyone to read it." She dropped the small book into the black schoolbag that she'd decorated with pink and yellow felt flower cutouts.

Next stop? The computer. Zee owed her BFF, Ally Stern, an IM.

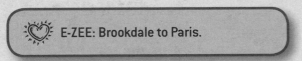

E-ZEE: Brookdale to Paris.

Actually, that was one thing that was not fantabsome about Zee's life. Zee and Ally had been BFFs since preschool. Then, over the summer, Ally announced that her parents, who were journalists, were moving their family to Paris, France. Zee missed her, but she liked hearing about Ally's new life—amazing French fashion, French food, and best of all, French boys—by IMing and emailing as much as possible.

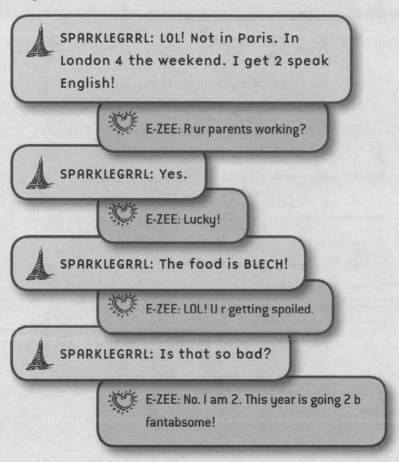

SPARKLEGRRL: LOL! Not in Paris. In London 4 the weekend. I get 2 speak English!

E-ZEE: R ur parents working?

SPARKLEGRRL: Yes.

E-ZEE: Lucky!

SPARKLEGRRL: The food is BLECH!

E-ZEE: LOL! U r getting spoiled.

SPARKLEGRRL: Is that so bad?

E-ZEE: No. I am 2. This year is going 2 b fantabsome!

SPARKLEGRRL: FANTABSOME???

 E-ZEE: I made it up. Like it?

 SPARKLEGRRL: What's it mean?

 E-ZEE: It means I'm going 2 b in a
REAL band, and I have THE BEST music
teacher on the planet.

 SPARKLEGRRL: LOL! U r so psyched.

 E-ZEE: Totally! Mr. P is a real rock star.

 SPARKLEGRRL: Have u 4gotten about
all the horrible stuff that happened
w K?

 E-ZEE: I have 2 4get—or at least 4give.
If I don't, the band won't work.

 SPARKLEGRRL: Good point!

E-ZEE: It's already going gr8. K and I r actually getting along.

 SPARKLEGRRL: Watch out! It could b a trick.

 E-ZEE: Mayb but it doesn't seem like 1.

 SPARKLEGRRL: Just b careful w K.

 E-ZEE: I will.

After the friends logged off, Zee unlocked her diary.

Ten Ways to Get Along with Kathi

Zee stared at the page, then struck through the first word.

Five
~~*Ten*~~ *Ways to Get Along with Kathi*

She tried again.

One Itty-Bitty, Teeny-Weeny
~~Five~~
~~Ten~~ Ways to Get Along with Kathi

Zee looked at the empty space on the page and sighed.
This is going to be harder than I thought!

Green with Envy

"Show your school spirit! Wear green on Friends' Day!" Two girls in cheerleading jerseys ran around the seventh-grade table, shaking their pom-poms.

"Hey! How come they don't have to wear uniforms?" Chloe asked. Zee's tweed Converse high-tops in blue plaid were the only difference between her outfit and Chloe's—a school-issued blue cotton vest and skirt and a white blouse.

"Official cheerleading business. They don't have to wear the school uniform on those days," Zee explained.

"Lucky them," Chloe said.

Jasper smoothed the front of his perfectly pressed navy-blue blazer. "Maybe you should become a cheerleader," he suggested.

"Naaaaah—I'd rather play soccer than cheer for it," Chloe told him.

Kathi's sister, Susan, was one of the cheerleaders. She was a taller, bouncier version of Kathi. Susan and the other cheerleader, Britney Zimmer, passed out fliers that read, *Think Green. Be a Friend of the Earth* across the top.

"What's Friends' Day?" Chloe asked the older girls.

"It's the first school spirit day of the year," Britney explained. "You don't have to wear your school uniform—as long as you wear something green—"

"Yuck!" Kathi interrupted. "I look horrible in green."

"It's just one day," Susan said cheerfully, "and it's a great way for all of Brookdale Academy to support the environment."

"You can be a friend to your friends, too," Britney said.

"How?" Marcus asked.

"You can make a card for a friend," Britney explained.

"Or a crush," Susan cut in.

"On recycled paper, of course," Britney added.

Jasper looked up from the cheese sandwich he was eating. "A crush?" he asked.

Susan leaned toward the group. "It's your chance to let someone know you're thinking about him—or her." She gave Jasper a nudge. He blushed and looked back down at his lunch. "Then come to the football game against Sprigg School," Susan continued, "and cheer the Brookdale Bears on to victory! Woo-hoo!" She and Britney bounced off to another table.

"I'm in!" Chloe shouted. "I'd wear a gorilla costume to get out of this thing," she added, tugging at her school-issued vest.

"I find the uniforms quite comfortable," Jasper said as

he buttoned his blazer. His striped tie hung perfectly straight.

Chloe shook her head. "Maybe we'll cast you as a business-man for the musical."

Jasper and Zee both laughed. But when Landon joined in, Jasper mumbled, "I guess some people prefer the baggy look."

Zee looked over at Chloe, who raised her eyebrow.

Landon picked up his fork and poked at the free-range chicken blob on his plate. "That was a really good idea to make it a rock-and-roll musical," he said to Zee.

Landon liked her idea! "Thanks," she said. *Good. Stop right there*, Zee told herself. *Be cool. Don't say any more.* "I just thought it would be cool beans if it were more than just a regular musical. I mean, we're a rock band, and Mr. P is in a rock band, so it makes sense. It's really obvious—if you think about it. Which I guess everyone did since they agreed to make it a rock musical." *Please. Stop. Now.* "Instead of a regular one."

Arrrrrgh! Zee screamed in her head. Why did she talk so much? She leaned toward Chloe and whispered, "Would you please take off one of your socks and shove it in my mouth?"

"I'm not wearing socks today," Chloe told her.

"Ohmylanta!"

"I like any kind of musical," Marcus said. *"Phantom of the Opera. The Lion King. Hairspray."*

Landon's eyes grew wide. "Are you messing with me?"

"What? There's nothing like a showstopping song," Marcus said.

Landon shook his head slowly. "I had no idea," he said.

As Zee laughed at Marcus and Landon, she peeled a long strip off her mozzarella string cheese and dropped it into her mouth.

Chloe squinted her green eyes and stared at Zee's face. "There's something on your chin," she said.

"What?" Zee asked, wiping her face. "Did I get it?"

"Nope," Chloe said.

Jasper looked up. "It's right—" he said, pointing to a spot on his own face, "there."

Zee furiously rubbed her chin.

"Hey! Where'd it go?" Marcus asked. "I was going to eat it."

"Ewwww!" Chloe said, but she was giggling.

Jasper laughed, too. "That's revolting," he said.

Phew! Zee let out a long breath, relieved that Marcus had taken the attention away from her.

"Ugh!" Kathi sighed dramatically. "You must be totally humiliated, Zee." Kathi sounded sympathetic, but Zee knew it was an act.

"Not really," Zee lied.

"I would be," Kathi said. "Luckily, nothing like that has ever happened to me." Kathi was too perfect to stumble, sputter, or—worst of all—leave food on her face.

"Would you like a crisp?" Jasper said, holding his bag

of potato chips up to Zee.

"Thanks," Zee said, smiling at him. Her mother never packed potato chips in her lunch, so she took a few. As she bit into one, she instantly felt better. He'd found the perfect way to change the subject.

Landon drummed out a beat on the table-top with his metal fork and spoon. "I hope we do something cool for the musical."

"Like what?" Zee asked.

"Maybe a musical about a bunch of students putting on a musical," Chloe suggested.

"Yawn," Jen said, closing her eyes and pretending to sleep.

"Jen's right," Kathi said. "*Everyone* does that."

"We could play ourselves," Marcus said.

Kathi rested her eyes on Jasper, who had started reading a book. "No offense, but *some people* might not be very interesting."

If Jasper got the insult, he didn't let on. "What about *Romeo and Juliet* set to music?" he suggested, raising his head. "We could update the story and make the characters our age."

"*Romeo and Juliet?*" Kathi asked. "I like it!"

"Really?" Zee said. It was impossible to guess when Kathi would be nice or nasty.

"Yeah," Kathi said, as if she were behaving normally.

"Me too," Jen agreed.

Chloe gave Jasper a firm pat on the back, and Marcus held up his hand high for Jasper to slap.

"I can definitely see myself playing Juliet," Kathi said.

Ohmylanta! Zee groaned to herself.

As much fun as the band was going to be, there was one important person missing—Ally. When Zee got home, she turned on her computer.

 E-ZEE: J came up w an idea 4 the musical. Every1 likes it.

 SPARKLEGRRL: Even K?

 E-ZEE: ESPECIALLY K. She plans 2 b the lead.

 SPARKLEGRRL: LOL! w L as the male lead?

E-ZEE: Probably!! LOL. Of course, I am planning 2 b the lead 2.

 SPARKLEGRRL: w L as the male lead?

 E-ZEE: LOL! Of course.

 SPARKLEGRRL: U r lucky. U have a big group 2 hang out w. I wish I did 2.

 E-ZEE: I thought u said u were making friends.

 SPARKLEGRRL: Yes—& no.

 E-ZEE: ???

 SPARKLEGRRL: People r nice 2 me, & we hang out. It's not like in CA, though. I had things in common w people there—even K. I don't know how 2 fit in here. There is 1 guy I like. We had pizza 2gether.

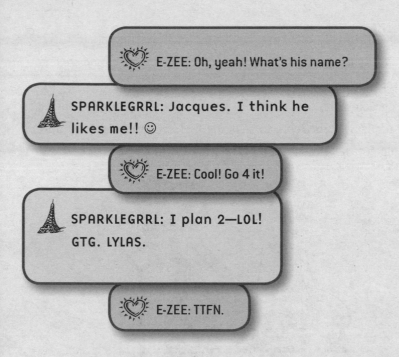

E-ZEE: Oh, yeah! What's his name?

SPARKLEGRRL: Jacques. I think he likes me!! ☺

E-ZEE: Cool! Go 4 it!

SPARKLEGRRL: I plan 2—LOL! GTG. LYLAS.

E-ZEE: TTFN.

Saturday morning Zee was helping Chloe and Jasper with their garden project. She stuck a shovel deep into a pile of dirt, then loaded the soil into the red wheelbarrow nearby and pushed it to where Chloe was kneeling in the garden bed.

"Where should I dump this?" Zee asked.

Chloe looked up. "Not here," she said, wiping her hands on the front of her denim overalls. "I'm all done."

Zee wiggled her toes in the navy-blue Converse sneakers

she'd pulled out of the back of her closet. She'd carefully chosen her garden-themed outfit—a pair of long blue shorts that she'd decorated with butterfly patches and belted with a green scarf, topped with a tank top and a pair of big blue sunglasses. She felt bad that she had been purposely avoiding getting as dirty as Chloe.

"You can dump the dirt over there," Chloe continued. She stood up and pointed to a plot where Jasper hoed the soil. "I'll help you guys."

Ms. Merriweather, the seventh-grade science teacher, tossed a big pile of dirt on to Jasper's plot. "Chloe and Jasper, you should be proud of yourselves," she said from underneath her giant, floppy straw hat. "Your science project is really shaping up."

"I feel as though we haven't done nearly enough," Jasper said.

"There will always be work to do," Ms. Merriweather said, "but you've accomplished a lot in a very short time. It's students like you that make Brookdale Academy a true LEED school." LEED stood for Leadership in Energy and Environmental Design and meant that Brookdale Academy was a green school.

"I knew composting the cafeteria scraps and planting vegetable gardens was a good idea," Chloe put in. "But I never realized it would be so much fun. Right, Zee?"

"Um . . . sure," Zee said. "I . . . uh . . . get to be with you guys. And I'm definitely getting stronger." She flexed her arms, pretending to show off muscles.

Chloe laughed. "It's probably a teeny bit more exciting when it's your own idea."

"Like the musical—well, mine and Kathi's and Jasper's," Zee said.

"Now *that's* going to be a lot of hard work," Jasper said.

Zee laughed. "That's the difference between us," she said. "Pushing around dirt is hard work to me. Planning a musical is fun. I'm going to ask if I can write the script, compose the music, work on the costumes, help Mr. P direct—"

"Hey! Between all of that and homework, you're not going to have any time for us," Chloe interrupted.

Zee reached out and put an arm around each of her friends' shoulders. "I'll *always* have time for you guys."

3

A Big Surprise

Zee's dad, J. P. Carmichael, turned his SUV around the corner toward Chloe's house. "What are you girls doing today?" he asked Zee.

"Working on *Taking Sides* with Jasper," Zee replied.

"Taking sides?" Zee's dad raised an eyebrow. "Against whom?"

Zee laughed. "*Taking Sides* is the name of the Beans' musical. Auditions are coming up."

"Oh, *that* explains all the singing in the shower."

"Yeah. Now I need a real audience."

"Which part are you trying out for?"

"Lily," Zee told him. "She's the female lead. Dylan is the male lead. They have two best friends named Brianna and

Gabe. And they spend a lot of time at the mall."

"I wonder who came up with that idea," Mr. Carmichael joked.

"An-y-way," Zee continued. "Lily's gang is a group of hip-hop dancers, and Dylan's friends are football players."

"And they all hang out together?"

"No way!" Zee said. "It's like *Romeo and Juliet*, so the groups totally don't get along. You know, they argue and make fun of each other. But then Lily and Dylan have a crush on each other, so things have to change."

"Hmmm . . . ," Mr. Carmichael said as he pulled into Chloe's driveway. "Problems with friends?"

"Yeah—and parents," Zee said. "Lily's mom and dad don't want her to date."

"I like it!" Mr. Carmichael cheered.

"Daaaad," Zee groaned as she climbed out of the SUV and grabbed her stars-and-stripes-studded guitar case.

Mr. Carmichael smiled and shrugged. "I'm just saying."

Zee shut the door. "Bye, Dad!" She was so excited, she climbed the Lawrence-Johnsons' steps by twos and rang the doorbell.

"Hello, Mackenzie." Chloe's mother greeted Zee with her soft southern accent. In her flowing silk pants, matching tank top, and strappy gold sandals, she looked as though she was dressed for a special dinner—not for a casual afternoon hanging out.

"Is Chloe here?" Zee asked.

"She's downstairs with Jasper," Mrs. Lawrence-Johnson said.

Zee bounded down the stairs to find Chloe and Jasper sitting on the couch next to the pool table.

"What about carrots?" Chloe said. "I like carrots."

"Me too," Jasper agreed, writing on his pad of paper.

"What are you guys doing?" Zee asked.

Chloe looked up. "We're just trying to figure out what to plant in the school garden."

"I thought we were going to practice for the musical," Zee said.

"We are," Chloe said. "But there are other things to think about."

"Not for me," Zee said.

"My mom says that if the band interferes with my schoolwork, I have to drop soccer—and I am *not* planning to do that," Chloe explained. "I just want a small role—like one of the hip-hop dancers."

"Well, *I* want to get the lead, so I need to start practicing," Zee said. "What about you, Jasper? Who do you want to be? Gabe? One of the gang?"

"Dylan, actually." He pushed his glasses up on his nose.

"What?" Zee's voice squeaked with surprise. Jasper could be shy, so she hadn't expected him to want the biggest part.

"You should *so* get that role," Chloe told Jasper.

"Really?" Jasper sat up a little straighter.

Zee slumped over. "Really?"

"Uh-huh," Chloe said to Jasper. "Nobody works harder than you do. You'd probably memorize all the lines in, like, a day."

"I do have an excellent memory," Jasper agreed.

"But Lily and Dylan are completely L.A.," Zee said. "I picture Dylan as a tanned surfer type."

Jasper looked suspicious. "That sounds a lot like Landon."

Why do I always let my mouth get me in trouble? "Oh, I didn't think of that," Zee said, trying to sound convincing. "Um . . . let's get started."

"Okay!" Chloe shot upright. "I'm gonna sing 'Love Story.' Good choice for a romantic musical, huh?"

"I'll play with you," Zee said, picking up her glittery guitar.

As Zee played, Chloe sang along. As usual, she sounded great. She had memorized all the words and hit every note perfectly—even though she was bouncing and spinning around the room. "'Romeo, save me, I've been feeling so alone,'" she belted, jumping up onto the couch, pretending to hold a microphone. When the song finished, she kicked her legs up in the air and plopped onto the cushion.

"Brilliant!" Jasper exclaimed.

"What did you think, Zee?" Chloe asked.

"You sounded amazing," Zee began. "But don't you want to practice the way you'll do it for the real audition? You won't be able to jump around."

Chloe flicked her hand in the air. "Nah," she said. "I'm just having fun."

Zee went to the brick hearth in front of the fireplace. "This is a good stage," she said, stepping up. With Jasper's and Chloe's eyes focused on her, Zee began to sing "Breaking Free" from *High School Musical*. Her voice trembled, and the first time she got to the chorus and sang "There's not a star in heaven that we can't reach," she couldn't hit the right notes. Then she forgot some of the words—even though she'd sung the song a million times. The more she messed up, the more nervous she got and the worse she did. She stopped singing. "That was a disaster!"

"It needs work," Chloe agreed. "Why are you so nervous? You've sung in front of people before."

"This audition is so important," Zee explained.

"I know what you mean," Jasper said, looking away.

"Okay, Jasper," Chloe said. "It's your turn. What are you gonna sing?"

"Something from *West Side Story*," he said. "But I'm not sure I know all the words." Jasper cleared his throat and nervously shifted his feet.

"Just sing the part you know. Then you can memorize the rest later," Chloe told him.

In the next beat, Jasper started to sing "Maria," a love ballad from the Broadway musical. Zee was shocked. Jasper was a great bass player, but she had never heard him sing before. His voice was strong and even. He had no problem hitting the highest notes—or the lowest ones. Had he been practicing as hard as Zee? Did he want the lead that much?

Then when Jasper sang "I just kissed a girl named Maria," Zee got a really weird feeling inside. She'd never heard him say anything so romantic.

"What's wrong?" Chloe asked her when Jasper had finished.

"What do you mean?" Zee asked.

"Your face is all white."

Zee reached up to her face. "I don't know what's wrong with me."

It was the truth. Because the problem was, *everything* was wrong.

* * *

5 Things I Know About Me

1. I HAVE to work really, really hard if I'm going to be Lily.
2. Landon has to be fantabsome if he is going to beat Jasper.
3. I'm not sure why I felt so weird around Jasper today.
4. I want Landon to beat Jasper— which means . . .
5. I am the worst friend in the world! ☹

4

Part Won

 E-ZEE: Audition 2morrow.

 SPARKLEGRRL: Good luck, Lily.

 E-ZEE: I BETTER get the part. I've been practicing CONSTANTLY. I am worried, though.

 SPARKLEGRRL: Y?

 E-ZEE: K wins everything.

SPARKLEGRRL: She didn't win *Teen Sing*—& that was the most important competition she has ever been in.

 E-ZEE: ☺ What's up in France?

 SPARKLEGRRL: Mom is interviewing Geneviève Lapointe next week at le Sentier. I get 2 go 2.

 E-ZEE: Who's that? And what's that?

 SPARKLEGRRL: She's a VERY famous French designer, and it's a really big fashion center.

 E-ZEE: Oh la la!

 SPARKLEGRRL: LOL!! Also, I'm officially going out w Jacques! ☺

 E-ZEE: Pizza Boy???

SPARKLEGRRL: Yes.

 E-ZEE: No way! Y didn't u tell me?

 SPARKLEGRRL: I just did!!! We went 2 the movies—and held hands!

 E-ZEE: Cool beans! I am totally jealous.

 SPARKLEGRRL: U won't b when u r going w L.

 E-ZEE: I hope, but I don't know if he'll EVER want 2 hold my hand.

 SPARKLEGRRL: 1st get the lead in the musical. THEN get the guy. That's how it is w real celebrities!

The next morning, Zee woke up early to practice lines with her mother.

"Did you hear that?" Mrs. Carmichael asked, looking around the kitchen.

"No, what?" Zee replied seriously.

"I think there's a burglar in the house."

"Do you want me to go look?" Zee stood up from the table.

Mrs. Carmichael grabbed her shoulder. *"No, it might not be safe,"* she whispered.

Thud. Thud. Thud. Zee's brother, Adam, sleepily crossed the room to the refrigerator. His wrinkled white Brookdale Academy shirt was untucked, and his tie hung loose around his neck.

Zee slapped her hands to her cheeks and let out a blood-curdling scream.

Adam flinched. "Thanks," he said. "I was hoping to lose some of my hearing this morning."

"Zee and I were just rehearsing for her audition today," their mother explained. "You look tired."

Adam opened the refrigerator door and searched the shelves. "Oh, I'm fine," he said. "Luckily, I don't actually need to sleep."

"Did you have trouble last night?" Mrs. Carmichael asked.

"Someone was up *very* early, singing in the shower," Adam grumbled.

He glared at Zee with sleepy eyes.

"Sorry," Zee apologized. "I didn't realize I was being so loud."

"I'll forgive you if you clean up my room this weekend."

"No way! Your room is revolting!" Zee said. "I'll have to live with you being mad at me forever."

"Well, the early-morning wake-up call doesn't really matter anyway," Adam said. "I've heard that song so many times, I've started singing it in my sleep."

"I'll be putting you out of your misery soon. Mr. P is casting the musical today."

"Good luck," Adam said. He grabbed a bagel and headed out of the kitchen, humming Zee's audition song.

Zee's mother sipped her tea. "Did you study for your test today?"

"A little," Zee said. "But I had to get ready for the audition. I'll do fine."

"You're taking the musical very seriously," Mrs. Carmichael said.

"Of course I am. I can't let the Beans down," Zee said, taking a swig of milk.

"Just remember, it's supposed to be fun," Mrs. Carmichael reminded her. "There are plenty of ways to show off your talents even if you're not the star."

"I know," Zee told her mother, then silently added,

But getting the lead is the only way to be sure Landon notices me.

"I'll be glad when this is over," Chloe said as she, Jasper, and Zee dodged the crush of students headed to first period.

"Me too," Jasper agreed. "I've been practicing for the audition nearly every moment I'm not working in the garden."

"You have?" Zee asked.

"Yes," Jasper said. "I was up late last night memorizing my lines."

"You were?" Zee said. "You know, you really didn't need to do that. Mr. P says you can read from the script."

"I know, but I thought it would sound more natural this way."

"Good thinking," Zee mumbled, hoping Landon had thought of that, too.

"You're going to be awesome, Jasper," Chloe cut in.

"He is?" Zee asked.

Chloe nudged Zee with her elbow. "You're asking too many questions," she said.

"I am?"

The three friends stepped into the music room. Zee's eyes zeroed in on Landon, who was reading his script.

The bell rang overhead.

"Okay, when everyone settles down, we'll get started," Mr. P announced. Zee, Chloe, and Jasper scrambled for seats. Zee found a chair in the front near the teacher.

Two men in blue jeans, with visitors' passes clipped to their shirts, walked into the classroom. One had dark brown hair with bangs and wore a blue plaid short-sleeve shirt. The other had blond hair that went every which way. He wore a plain white T-shirt.

"These are the other members of my band, the Crew," Mr. P announced. "They're going to help me with the casting."

As her teacher spoke, Zee twisted her neck and looked at the faces behind her. Jen and Landon looked scared. Kathi and Jasper looked confident. And Chloe and Marcus looked somewhere in between.

"Zee, you can go first," Mr. P said.

Ugh! "Me?" Zee gulped.

"Sure," Mr. P said. "We'll just go around the room in order. No big deal."

What had Zee been thinking? *Even a first grader knows to sit in the back if you don't want to get picked first.*

Zee stood. "Here? In front of everyone?" she asked.

"No, you'll go to one of the soundproof practice rooms where only the judges will hear you," Mr. P explained. "Kathi, will you please lead the others in scales and warm-ups?"

Kathi tilted her head and rolled her eyes in fake embarrassment as she walked to the front of the room.

Mr. P looked at the class. "When it's your turn to audition, please come to practice room one," he said, then turned to Zee. "Ready?"

No, Zee thought, but she knew she couldn't say it. "Yes." As she stood, Chloe gave her a thumbs-up and Jasper flashed a smile.

Then Landon looked up. "Good luck," he said.

"Thanks!" *Now* Zee was ready. Until she glanced at Kathi. The fire in her eyes could have burned a hole through Zee's uniform. Zee quickly looked away and followed the Crew into the hall. Her heart pounded in her ears.

"Which part will you be trying out for?" Mr. P asked once they got to the audition room.

"The lead. Lily."

Mr. P wrote on a blank piece of paper. "Go ahead and start your audition song whenever you're ready."

"Hm mm mm." Zee cleared her throat. She was so nervous that when she opened her mouth, she wasn't sure what would come out. But all of her practice paid off. When she sang, the music took over. Before she'd really had a chance to worry, she'd reached the end of the song.

The judges silently scribbled some notes on their papers. Finally, Mr. P said, "Great! Now let's run through the scene. I'll be the scared roommate."

The pages in Zee's hands shook, and she wished she had memorized the lines like Jasper had. Luckily, her voice covered up the noise of the paper, and she read the script just like she'd practiced with her mother.

"Very impressive!" the blond Crew member said when she finished.

"You liked it?"

"Yeah," Mr. P's other bandmate said.

"You can go back and send in the next person," Mr. P told her.

"Cool beans!" Zee said. With a skip, she hurried back to the music room.

Jen and Marcus took their turns. Then Chloe practically sprinted out of the room for her audition.

"How'd it go?" Zee asked when her friend returned.

"I dunno," Chloe said, "but it was fun."

Landon was next. "Break a leg!" Zee said as he walked by her desk.

"Could everyone please pay attention to the concert-mistress?" Kathi barked.

Zee tried to play the scales on her guitar, but it was hard to concentrate. What if Landon didn't even want to be the lead? What if he messed up? What if Landon *did* get the lead—but so did Kathi?

Finally, Landon returned.

Is he happy? Zee wondered. She couldn't tell.

"Ahem." Jasper got Zee's attention. He was standing next to her.

"What's up?" Zee asked. Chloe gestured wildly and mouthed something Zee couldn't understand.

"Aren't you going to wish me luck?" Jasper asked.

"Oh, yeah!" Zee said, snapping out of her Landon-induced trance. "Definitely. Good luck. Knock 'em dead."

"Thanks," Jasper said, looking down at his feet as he walked away.

Chloe slowly shook her head back and forth.

"What?" Zee asked, shrugging.

"Oh . . . nothing," Chloe said.

When Jasper came back, he was beaming. "Mr. P said he hardly recognized me, because I got into the character so much," Jasper exclaimed.

"It would be so cool if you got to play Dylan," Chloe said and gave him a high five.

"Especially if Zee could be my costar, Lily," Jasper agreed.

"Yeah, that would be great," Zee said, wondering if she sounded as fake as she felt.

Kathi put down her conductor's baton and headed toward the door for her turn. "What if you and Kathi are the leads?" Chloe asked Jasper.

Jasper shuddered and Chloe laughed.

Mr. P stuck his head around the door. "Kathi is the last to audition, and the period is almost over," he said to the rest of the class. "You guys can just hang for a while. After Kathi finishes, I'll post the cast list."

The other students began talking about their auditions. While no one was looking, Zee took out her diary and began writing.

Hi, Diary,

My audition went really well, but I'm having a minor freakout. What if Jasper and I are the leads? He's one of my very best friends. It would be weird to pretend we're boyfriend and girlfriend.

Horrible Things That Are Still Better Than Pretending to Be Your Best Friend's Girlfriend

1. Having a face full of freckles that make you look 7 years old.
2. Having no boobs. None. Nada.
3. Having food hanging from your face in front of the cutest guy in school (Landon!).

Since all of those things have already happened to me, I think I deserve some good luck. Plus, I'm sure Jasper would be sooooo uncomfortable, too. So I guess I'm not totally evil if I hope only one of us gets the lead. It's for his sake, too.

Zee

Zee slipped her diary inside her music folder just as Mr. P appeared at the front of the room.

"Hey, everyone!" Mr. P got the class's attention. "The Crew was really impressed with each of you." Beside him, his bandmates nodded. "I've posted the results in the hallway beside the door. And remember that the casting has nothing to do with who's best—it's about who's best for each role."

Kathi huffed with laughter. "That's what they all say."

The bell rang overhead, and Zee sprang out of her seat. "I've booked the school auditorium for the show," Mr. P shouted over the noisy rush of students, each hurrying to be the first out of the room. "So we've got just a few weeks to create an original musical from start to finish."

Kathi was the first one to the list. "Aaaaaaaah!" she screeched.

"What is it?" Jen asked, hurrying to her side.

"I'm the sidekick, Brianna," Kathi said to Jen. "The lead's sidekick is a nothing part."

"Who's Lily?" Jen asked.

"Zee."

"All right!" Chloe said, giving Zee a quick hug.

Of course, Zee was happy, but playing Kathi's best friend was going to take more than great acting. It would take a miracle to pull that off.

Then the news got even worse for Kathi—and better for Zee. "Landon is Dylan," Marcus pointed out. By now, everyone was crowded around the list.

"And Jasper is Gabe, Dylan's sidekick," Chloe said.

"Cool beans!" Zee said. "Dylan's best friend. That's a majorly important part."

"I suppose," Jasper sighed, and turned to a smiling Chloe, who was part of Lily's girl group with Jen. "You look awfully happy."

"I am," Chloe told him. "I was worried I'd get a big part and wouldn't have enough time for soccer and the gardening project."

"There's still a lot of work for everyone to do—on the scripts, the music, stage crew—" Zee reminded her.

"Boy, I sure am glad *you're* not the teacher," Chloe said,

cutting her off. "You'd have us working twenty-four hours a day." She grabbed Zee's arm and began to drag her down the hall. "Now let's go so we're not late for English. We've got classes besides music, you know."

The girls said good-bye to Jasper and headed down the hall. Suddenly, Zee realized what had just happened. *I am actually going to be the romantic lead in a musical with Landon!*

"Hi, best friend!" Kathi cheerfully greeted Zee at lunch. Usually, she sat between Jen and Landon, but that afternoon she planted herself next to Zee.

Jasper choked on his egg salad sandwich, and Zee knocked over her banana-mango smoothie. Chloe simultaneously handed Jasper a bottle of water and tossed a couple of napkins over the thick yellow liquid that spread across the table.

"What did you say?" Zee asked Kathi. She looked around for hidden cameras.

"Yeah," Jen said. "*What* did you say?"

"I'm talking about the musical," Kathi said, tossing her hair over her shoulder. "You know—Lily and Brianna. Best friends. Maybe Lily will get Brianna a Friends' Day surprise. Hint, hint."

"I kinda wasn't sure how you'd feel about getting that part," Zee said.

"Why? Because I won't be the star?" Kathi asked. "No prob." She casually scooped a spoonful of yogurt. "When we work on the script, we can fix that."

"Fix it?" Chloe asked suspiciously.

"Duh!" Kathi said. "By making sure I have enough lines."

Zee took a deep breath. She wanted to scream, "But you're not the star! *I* am!"

Landon stepped in. "Umm . . . ," he said, looking from Kathi to Zee and nervously drumming out a beat on the table with his fingers. "Maybe we should start planning what everyone's going to do."

"Is that really necessary?" Jasper asked.

"What do you mean?" Landon responded. His hands stopped drumming.

"I'd rather not spend my lunch talking about the musical." Jasper peeled his orange.

"Well, we do have a lot to get done before the show," Zee said.

Jasper looked at Zee as if she'd just punched him in the nose. "That doesn't mean we have to talk about it *constantly*."

"It would be cool to come up with a few ideas for the sets, costumes, and music so everyone knows what they want to work on," Marcus said.

"Marcus is right," Jen chimed in quickly.

Chloe was more concerned about Jasper. "It's okay if you just wanna hang out and listen," she assured her friend.

Zee worried that Jasper was feeling ganged up on, too, but she'd never seen him like this. He sounded really angry—not like him at all. Was he actually mad at Landon for getting the lead?

"Why don't we meet at the Brookdale Mall Café tomorrow to talk about ideas?" Zee suggested.

Unfortunately, Zee wasn't exactly sure how that would solve her problem. Even though Kathi was pretending to be best friends with Zee, Jasper couldn't even be friendly with Landon. This was not how things were supposed to go—at all.

5

Part Too

 E-ZEE: Major news!

 SPARKLEGRRL: U got the lead!

 E-ZEE: How did u know?

 SPARKLEGRRL: It was on the news in Paris.

 E-ZEE: Really?

 SPARKLEGRRL: Yes, and did u know that *gullible* isn't in the dictionary?

E-ZEE: Really?

 SPARKLEGRRL: No, I made up both things. This is way 2 easy.

 E-ZEE: U should b nice so I'll tell u the REALLY big news.

 SPARKLEGRRL: L's the other lead?

 E-ZEE: R u psychic?

 SPARKLEGRRL: Pretty much. Congrats! U r going 2 b an awesome Lily!!!

 E-ZEE: The band is going 2 the mall 2day.

 SPARKLEGRRL: Have fun. I have a date 2nite avec mon amour.

 E-ZEE: Jacques?

 SPARKLEGRRL: Who else? I think he might kiss me.

Wow! Ally was going to have her first kiss, and Zee was excited just to be cast in a play with her crush. She didn't even know if Landon liked her. She and Ally weren't just living thousands of miles apart. They were light-years apart when it came to boys, too.

"Remind me again why your dad dropped us off," Jasper asked Zee at the mall. "We had enough time to ride our bikes."

Zee thought fast, then looked at Jasper. "Today's a big deal. You're getting your first pair of sneakers," she said. "I didn't want you to be too tired to shop."

"Just wait until you actually get blue jeans," Chloe said and laughed. "We might ride to the mall in a limousine."

Jasper fiddled with the button at the top of his brown polo shirt and grinned. "Aww, that's nice," he said. "But I know you hate riding in your father's SUV, because it uses so much gas."

Jasper was right, but a bike was out of the question. There was no way Zee was going to show up sweaty with her hair in windblown knots in front of Landon! But she decided her friends didn't need to know the *whole* truth. So she just said, "If we all buy stuff, it'll be hard to get everything home on our bikes." Then she quickly looked around the shoe store, hoping to change the subject. "So, which sneakers do you like, Jasper?" She reached for a plain black skate shoe on the shelf in front of her.

"Do *you* like that one?" Jasper asked.

Zee shrugged. "Sure. Do you?"

"If you do."

"How about this style?" Chloe asked. She pointed to a gray-and-red shoe on the table in front of her.

"Which do you like better?" Jasper asked Zee.

"That one." Zee nodded toward the sneaker Chloe had selected. "Or this one," she added, picking up a white tennis shoe.

Panic took over Jasper's face. "You like them *both*?"

"Yeah. I have about ten pairs of shoes, and I like them all."

Jasper spotted a pair of blue canvas Converse just like Zee's. "Oh, look," he said. "I could get a pair just like yours."

Zee shook her head. "I think your feet are too long. They'd just end up looking like clown shoes."

Jasper grabbed the side of his head and looked from shoe to shoe to shoe.

"I think Jasper needs your help making a decision," Chloe suggested.

"Oh, okay," Zee said. "Maybe you could try on a couple of pairs and see how they look."

Jasper asked the saleswoman to get two pairs in his size. He laced up a different shoe on each foot and stood. "What do you think?"

"I like that pair," Zee told him, pointing to the style Chloe had picked out. She turned to Chloe.

"Uh-huh," Chloe agreed. "That's my vote, too."

"Really? Are they cool?" Jasper asked.

"Since when do you care about cool?" Zee asked.

"It's . . . uh . . . a recent development."

"They're very cool," Zee told him. "You should wear them right now."

Jasper smiled. "I will!" he said and paid for his new shoes.

"Do I look American?" Jasper asked.

"Well . . . hmmm . . . ummm." Zee hesitated.

"Not hardly," Chloe said. She turned around in a circle.

"Do you see anyone else with a collared shirt and a *belt*?"

"I guess it will take more than just new trainers," Jasper said.

"You really do look good," Zee told him.

Jasper turned bright red as a grin spread across his face. "Thanks! I guess my feet just needed a makeover."

Zee's Sidekick beeped. A text message from Marcus.

>We r here. R u?

Zee looked at the time on her phone. "Ohmylanta!" she groaned. "We're late." The girls grabbed Jasper and headed to the café.

Zee ordered a frozen mocha drink, Jasper opted for tea,

and Chloe chose vitamin water. As they got near the table, Marcus was standing up and taking charge of the group.

"You started without us?" Zee asked, sitting in an empty chair next to him and pulling a notepad out of her bag.

"Yeah," Marcus said. "We weren't sure when you'd get here."

"Oh, okay," Zee said. "I had a few ideas about—"

"We just started picking jobs," Marcus interrupted. "I can work on sets."

"Me too," Chloe said, sliding into a chair.

Zee wrote down the assignments in her notebook.

"I think it would be fun to do props," Jen said. She spooned some of the whipped cream topping from her drink into her mouth.

"Boring!" Zee whispered to Jasper.

"Props sounds cool," Landon said.

"Yeah!" Zee had a sudden change of heart. "I'll do props, too."

Kathi whipped her head around to face Zee. "That's too many people for props."

"Yes, far too many," Jasper agreed.

Zee was embarrassed because Kathi and Jasper were right. And Zee was certain it was obvious to everyone that she'd volunteered just to be with Landon. "Ummm . . . I meant to say I'd do costumes."

"Perfect!" Kathi said. "We can make the costumes together."

"You and me?" Zee asked.

"Best friends!"

"*Ri-ight,*" Zee said suspiciously.

"Jasper, what are you going to do?" Landon asked.

"I haven't decided yet," Jasper said without looking at Landon.

"Well, we *kind of* need to know," Zee said gently. "We're trying to get organized."

Jasper looked at Zee. "Mr. P will need an assistant director," he said. "I could do that."

"Dude, you'd be perfect," Landon said. He leaned over and sucked soda through his straw.

"Why do you say that . . . *dude?*" Jasper asked.

Landon shrugged. "I guess 'cause your accent is kind of cool—like Shakespeare's."

"Yes, I suppose that makes me the best qualified," Jasper said sarcastically.

Whoa! Zee thought. *Jasper's never sarcastic.*

But when Landon laughed, everyone else did, too. And even Jasper smiled at his own snarky remark.

"We'll all write the script together," Chloe said.

"And Mr. P said he'd work with everyone on the songs," Zee added.

"Okay, that covers sets, props, costumes, the assistant director, the script, and the songs. I guess we're done," Marcus said.

Everyone else stood up and started to leave.

"Wait!" Zee called out. "Where's everyone going? We're just getting started."

"My cousin is having her fifteenth birthday today," Jen said. "I have to get ready for her quinceañera. Kathi's coming, too!"

"Chloe?" Zee said.

"Jasper and I should go, too. Ms. Merriweather is helping us plant the vegetable plot today."

"Landon?" Zee asked hopefully.

"My dad is taking me to get a new surfboard."

Zee looked at Marcus, who smiled back at her. "Aren't you going to ask me?" he inquired.

"Should I even bother?" Zee said.

"Probably not. UCLA is giving my mom an award. My whole family is going."

Zee closed her notebook. Her ideas for the music and choreography would just have to wait.

* * *

As soon as she got home, Zee raced up to her room to IM Ally. But when she logged on, Ally was offline. So she typed an email instead.

> A,
> OMG! Everything is all mixed up. Kathi is being
> nice (mostly) and Jasper is acting totally weird.
> Not to me. To Landon. I guess he's mad because
> he worked so hard to get the lead. He's also really
> getting into fashion—or at least trying to. All he
> used to care about was books, soccer, and the
> environment. What's up with him?
> And where r u?
> BFF, Z

Ally's response arrived later.

> Z,
> Please don't tell me ur going 2 b K's friend again.
> DO NOT FORGET WHAT SHE DID WITH YOUR
> DIARY!!!!!! She is so 2-faced. U can't trust her.

How could Ally be so sure about Kathi? Ally wasn't there, so she couldn't see how Kathi was acting. Was it so crazy to think that Kathi might actually like Zee? *People can change*, Zee thought and read on.

> Jacques and I took a walk along the Seine River.
> Guess what? He says I'm his g/f! I'm sending you
> a pic of him (with me!) so you can see how cute he
> is.
> LYLAS,
> Ally

Zee stared at the photo of her BFF and the stranger. Jacques *was* cute, but he had straight dark hair and a serious face. When Ally lived in California, she always had crushes on blond boys.

But the biggest difference between Brookdale Ally and Paris Ally might be free time. Now that she had a boyfriend, would Ally be there for Zee?

Identity Crisis

Zee's fingers typed quickly in the glow of the computer screen under her comforter.

> Lily: Come on, guys! We're going to be late for the football game.
> Brianna: Why are you so interested in football? You never cared about it before.
> Lily: I guess I changed my mind.

Mr. P had set up a blog for the Beans, so they could share scenes, songs, pictures, and videos. Zee was eager to get as much done as possible. Getting the script right was so important.

Click. Zee's door opened.

"Zee?"

Busted! Zee closed her laptop and peeked out from under the covers. "Yes, Mom?" she said as cheerfully as she could manage.

"Why are you still awake?" Mrs. Carmichael asked. "Are you doing homework?"

Zee looked at the clock, which flashed 11:37. "Sort of."

Mrs. Carmichael crossed her arms. "Go on," she said skeptically. "I'm listening."

"We're nearly finished with the script for the musical," Zee explained. "I was just working on one of my scenes so it will be perfect."

"I'm sure it can wait." Mrs. Carmichael bent over and took the laptop. "You'll do better when you're rested anyway."

Zee pulled her covers up to her chin. "Good night, Mom," she said, although she was certain all the thoughts spinning in her head would keep her awake.

In study hall the next day, Kathi tapped furiously on the class computer. "What do you think?" she asked when she finished.

Zee read the script out loud. *"Dylan leans toward Lily. Slowly, his face moves closer to hers."* Zee's heart pounded. *"Just as their lips are about to meet,"* Zee continued, *"Brianna appears and stops them.*

"Ummm . . . that doesn't seem realistic to me," Zee said. "Wouldn't Brianna be happy for her friend—you know, that she's going to kiss the boy she likes?"

Kathi shook her head. "No way," she said. "It's just like *Romeo and Juliet.* Brianna knows their crush is doomed, so she's keeping them apart for her friend's own good."

Zee was suspicious. "Are you sure it's not because her best friend is *jealous*?"

"I'm sure. No one was jealous in *Romeo and Juliet.*"

"I guess you're right," Zee mumbled.

* * *

After the final period of the day, Zee met Chloe at her locker.

"I've got a *ton* of homework," Chloe said, looking lopsided under the weight of her homemade patchwork book bag.

Zee looked at her assignment book. "Me too," she said. "Math, science, *and* French. Plus, we have that English quiz tomorrow."

"Are you still coming over to my house to study for it?" Chloe asked.

"Yup. I told my mom I would go home from school with you." Zee grabbed her books out of her locker and shoved them into her bag. The lockers were made of recycled wheat board, so the door made a soft *thud* when she shut it.

Zee could barely lug her heavy bag down the hall. She hadn't gotten far with Chloe when she spotted Landon approaching.

Great! Zee groaned silently. *Just when I'm looking like the Hunchback of Notre Dame. Maybe he won't see me.* She looked at the ground in the opposite direction.

"Hey, Zee!" Landon called out.

Darn it! Zee stood up as straight as she could. "Oh, hi, Landon," she said, trying to sound casual. "What's up?"

"Mr. P just told me he wants us to work on the scene

where Lily and Dylan first meet," Landon began. "Do you have time now?"

"Sure."

"But we were going to study for the English test," Chloe reminded her.

"It's just a quiz," Zee said. "Landon and I won't take long. I'll come over in an hour."

Chloe adjusted her book bag strap on her shoulder. "All right. It'll probably take me that long to drag this thing out of the building," she said.

"You're not going anywhere," Mr. P boomed, grabbing Zee's arm. *"I'm calling the police!"*

"Let go of me!" Zee yelled, trying to break free from her teacher's grip. Mr. P was playing a store owner who accuses Lily of shoplifting.

"Halt!" Landon protested loudly. "Uhh. Ummm. Eh." He heaved a sigh and threw up his hands. "I have no idea what to say."

"Don't sweat it, Landon," Mr. P reassured him. "What would you say if it happened in real life? Just pretend you're really Dylan, and you need to convince me to let Lily go."

Landon looked at Zee. *"Let her go!"* he shouted, getting into character.

"Why? What's it to you?" Mr. P snarled. Zee tried not to giggle. She didn't want to ruin Landon's concentration.

"Because I know she would never steal anything," Landon went on. "I can tell just by looking at her. I've never seen such an honest face in my life."

Zee could feel a blush fill her cheeks.

"All right," Mr. P said, releasing his grasp. "But if I ever see either one of you in my store again, I'm going to call mall security." Then Mr. P turned into their teacher again. "See? You rocked it."

"Cool." Landon flipped his bangs back with a flick of his head.

"You guys are off to a good start," Mr. P said. "Why

don't you try revising the rest of the scene on your own? Then show me."

"Ahem." Kathi cleared her throat. She'd been in the room the whole time. Zee could see she'd put on a fresh coat of lip gloss while they'd been practicing.

Ohmylanta! Here it comes! Zee thought. She knew Kathi's good behavior had been too good to be true. Now what was she going to do to sabotage Zee's time with Landon?

"If you guys don't need Mr. P's help anymore," Kathi continued, "I have a few questions for him."

"We're done," Landon said to Kathi. Then he turned to Zee. "Do you want to work on this some more?"

Zee stopped herself from screaming, "Fantabsome! You want to hang out alone with me? Cool beans!" Instead she super-casually said, "Sure."

As Zee and Landon worked on the script at one of the computers in the back of the music room, Zee couldn't help overhearing Kathi's questions. "Which scenes am I supposed to write?" "What date is the performance?" "Are we going to sell tickets?" Mr. P answered all of them— even though he had already posted all of the information on the blog.

Landon pointed to the computer screen. "Here Dylan

could say something like, 'I've never met anyone like you.'"
Landon turned and his blue eyes stared intensely at Zee.

"You're a great writer, Dylan."

"Huh?" Landon said.

"Umm . . . I said, 'That's great, Landon.'"

"You called me Dylan."

"Did I?"

A beep from Zee's Sidekick interrupted them. A text from Chloe.

>R u coming?

Oh, no! Zee had completely forgotten. She was supposed to be at Chloe's house to study for the English quiz! She looked from her Sidekick to Landon. She couldn't stop now.

>I am sooooooo sorry. I 4got.

>K.

Zee was relieved that Chloe wasn't mad. She'd make it up to her.

* * *

E-ZEE: How do u know if a guy likes u?

 SPARKLEGRRL: Y?

 E-ZEE: I think L might like me.

 SPARKLEGRRL: Really? Did he say something?

 E-ZEE: Yes. We were writing a scene & he kept saying really romantic stuff.

 SPARKLEGRRL: But isn't it the character Dylan saying that?

 E-ZEE: Yes, but L is thinking it.

 SPARKLEGRRL: It's definitely a clue.

 E-ZEE: I hope so.

 SPARKLEGRRL: Mayb u'll have a b/f soon 2!!! Then we'll b =.

 E-ZEE: Yeah.

Hi, Diary,

Ally said something weird that's kind of bothering me. Does she really think that we're not equal—that she's better than me? That's not like her—or the old Ally, at least. But the old Ally didn't have a boyfriend.

The thing is, I wish Landon was my boyfriend. Ally has only been in France a few months, and she has Jacques. What am I doing wrong? I've known Landon since kindergarten.

Zee

* * *

"Maybe I should get him some cologne," Zee said, heading toward the perfume counter at the mall the next weekend. It was Brookdale Academy's fall break, which meant four days off. Zee was glad to have the time to work on the script and a few new songs, but she'd been so focused on the musical, she'd nearly forgotten her dad's birthday.

Chloe scrunched up her face. "Cologne? For your dad's birthday? That's not very original."

"I know, but I'm desperate." Zee picked up a tiny bottle. But before she could squirt herself, Chloe grabbed it away.

"No, not that one. They test on animals." She placed a new bottle in Zee's empty hand.

"I waited until the last minute," Zee said as she sprayed her wrist, then gave it a sniff. "Mom is *so* not happy. She wanted everyone to give Dad his presents at his birthday breakfast this morning, but I've been working so hard on the musical, I haven't had a chance to get him anything."

Zee sighed and turned to Jasper. "What do you think I should get my dad?" she asked. "You're a guy."

"Thank you for noticing," Jasper said, shuffling his feet. He was still getting used to his new sneakers.

Zee rolled her eyes. "You know what I mean."

Jasper adjusted his glasses. "Tickets to a Galaxy

game?" he suggested.

"Soccer?" Zee asked. "Dad's not a big fan."

"Your dad will like whatever you get for him," Jasper said. "You don't have to make a big deal out of it."

"That's it!" Zee shouted.

"What?" Jasper asked, confused.

"I should *make* something for him."

"Did I say that?" Jasper asked.

Chloe shrugged. "Only sort of. But it doesn't matter. It's a great idea."

"Like decorate a picture frame," Zee suggested.

"Awesome! I'll make one for my mom, too. Her birthday is in two weeks," Chloe added.

"Cool beans!" Zee said. "You want to join us, Jasper? We can talk about your part in the musical."

"I'd rather not be reminded," Jasper declined.

What's up with Jasper? Zee wondered. Then her Sidekick beeped with a text. "Darn it!"

"What?" Chloe asked.

Zee showed the screen to Chloe.

>Can't. My family's @ our cabin in Tahoe over break.

"Landon's family went out of town for break. I asked

him to rehearse with me," Zee said. "I have so many lines to learn. I'm afraid I'll never get them all memorized in time unless I practice every day."

Jasper began to walk slightly ahead of the girls.

"You've got some big scenes with Jasper, too," Chloe pointed out. "Why don't you run lines with him?"

"That's a good idea!" Zee said. Then she called to him, "Will you help me, Jasper?"

"That would be brilliant," Jasper told her. "And I think I *will* make prezzies with you. My nana's coming for a visit from England soon. She'd love a homemade frame with a picture of her favorite grandson."

"Aren't you her only grandson?" Chloe asked.

"You don't have to nitpick," Jasper said, smiling.

Chloe IMed Zee after dinner.

 SOCCERNOW: Did ur dad like his present?

 E-ZEE: Yes, but it was still a little wet when I gave it 2 him.

 SOCCERNOW: I think this was J's 1st time using glue.

E-ZEE: LOL! His was kinda messy. . . .
He's been acting weird.

It took Chloe a while to respond.

 SOCCERNOW: What do u mean?

 E-ZEE: It's like he gets mad at me 4 no
reason.

 SOCCERNOW: That doesn't sound like
him.

 E-ZEE: I know. That's what's strange.

7

The New Girl (and Boy)

 SPARKLEGRRL: Bonjour!

 E-ZEE: Hey!

 SPARKLEGRRL: How was ur long weekend?

 E-ZEE: Good. I practiced 4 the musical w J. We've still got A LOT 2 learn!

 SPARKLEGRRL: J? Y not L?

E-ZEE: He went away 4 break. PLUS I still have no idea if he likes me.

 SPARKLEGRRL: I just got my new Flip mag. There's a whole article about how 2 tell if a guy likes u.

 E-ZEE: 411 pls.

 SPARKLEGRRL: It's all stuff about body language. Like does he touch his hair when u get close?

 E-ZEE: He does!

Zee's heart pounded at the thought.

 SPARKLEGRRL: Does he make up excuses to call and email u?

Hmmmm.

 E-ZEE: No.

SPARKLEGRRL: That doesn't mean anything all by itself. There's a whole list. I'll fax it 2 u.

 E-ZEE: U r the best!!!!

 SPARKLEGRRL: LYLAS!!

Zee ran downstairs to her father's home office where the fax machine was already humming. She grabbed the pages and picked up a pen off the nearby cherrywood desk. She headed back to her room and curled up in her comfy chair where she focused on the quiz questions.

    1. *Does he touch his hair when you're nearby?*
        a. Yes.
        b. Sometimes.
        c. No.

Zee circled *a*.

    2. *Does he sit next to you at lunch?*

a. Yes.

b. Sometimes.

c. No.

Sometimes, Zee thought, but the whole music class can say that—except Kathi, who got to circle *a*.

3. When you turn his way, is he looking at you?

No. That wasn't going to help her score, but it was true.

Zee went through the rest of the questions.

4. Does he stumble or drop things when you're around?

5. Does he stammer when he talks to you?

Zee circled *sometimes* for those two and for most of the remaining questions. Then she totaled her answers and checked her score. "Inconclusive," she read. "It's hard to tell if your cutie is crushing on you or not. But keep an eye on him to see how things develop."

"Ohmylanta!" Zee said out loud. She took out her diary.

3 Reasons I'll Be Happy Break Is Over

1. Getting to see Landon again.

2. Getting to see if Landon likes me!

3. Getting to work on the musical.
   (With Landon, of course.) ☺

* * *

"Wait up!" Chloe called out to Zee, who was speed walking to first period. "I can hardly keep up with you."

"Sorry," Zee said, stopping so her friend could walk beside her. "I'm just so excited, because"—she paused—"after four days away, I'm ready to get to work on *Taking Sides*."

"You're not going to be able to sing a note if you're winded," Chloe pointed out as the girls rounded the corner and entered the room.

"That's why I want to get there. . . ." Zee's voice trailed off.

Two unfamiliar figures stood at Mr. P's desk—a girl with a teddy bear backpack purse and a tall boy with his hair spiked up on top. They both wore Brookdale Academy uniforms.

Landon entered the room, too. *Yay!* Zee thought, smiling in his direction. Landon didn't notice. His eyes were glued on the new girl.

As Landon reached up to smooth down the hair on top of his head, Zee remembered the magazine quiz she'd taken the day before. *"Does he touch his hair when you're nearby?"* Ugh!

The girl stopped talking to Mr. P and turned around. She was incredibly pretty, with silky, shiny brown hair and a button nose. Her dark eyes were circled by long eyelashes. She looked at Landon, who was staring right at her.

"When you turn his way, is he looking at you?" Zee remembered another question from the quiz. This super-pretty student could definitely circle *yes*.

As Landon headed to his seat, he tripped. *"Does he stumble or drop things when you're around?"* Yikes! It just got worse and worse.

Ohmylanta! Zee's heart felt like someone were stomping on it. Having perfect Kathi around to steal Landon's attention had been bad enough. Now there was this new girl. Was she going to ruin everything for Zee—right at the moment Zee was beginning to think Landon really might like her back?

Jasper turned Zee's way and grinned. "What?" Zee whispered.

"It looks like Landon might have a thing for the new girl."

Zee sighed. If Jasper had noticed, Zee knew she was in trouble.

The new girl accidentally bumped Zee's leg with her violin case. "Oh, I'm such a klutz. Are you okay?" she apologized, giving Zee a sweet smile. A *real* one. Now Zee felt even worse. The girl couldn't help the fact that she was so pretty. And if she was nice, who cared what she looked like?

Chloe elbowed Zee out of her thoughts and gestured to the new boy, who high-fived Marcus, then sat down next to him. The new boy put his sax case on the floor.

Marcus looked at the other students, who were staring at him. "Oh. This is Conrad. We met at the music store this weekend," he explained. "Then we hung out."

Landon's mouth dropped open. It was obvious he had no idea Marcus had made a new friend over break.

Chloe wiggled her eyebrows up and down at the boy. Zee had to admit, with his dark eyes and spiky hair, he was cute—not gorgeously handsome like Landon, of course, but cute.

"Listen up, everyone," Mr. P said, quieting down the students. "We lucked out and got two additions to the class. This is Missy Vasi," he said, nodding toward the girl, "and Conrad Mitori," he added, tilting his head in the other direction. "The timing is perfect. Over the break I realized that our leads don't have understudies. Missy and Conrad have agreed to learn those parts and fill in if necessary."

"You mean, they won't get to be in the musical unless Zee or Landon can't play their parts?" Kathi asked. "That doesn't seem fair."

"Good point," Mr. P said.

A huge smile spread across Kathi's face as she proudly looked around the room. "Thanks!"

"We could use more people in Lily's and Dylan's groups of friends," Mr. P began, "so Missy and Conrad would be great there."

"Would it be okay if Conrad and I worked on mixing music, too?" Marcus asked. "Missy could take my place on sets."

"That would be awesome," Missy said. "I love to do scenery."

"Yes!" said Conrad. "DJ Conrad's in the house!"

Everyone laughed—especially Jasper. Zee thought he looked happier than he had in a while.

***

 E-ZEE: New girl alert!

 SPARKLEGRRL: 411???!!!!

 E-ZEE: Her name is Missy. She's nice.

 SPARKLEGRRL: Good.

 E-ZEE: Smart.

 SPARKLEGRRL: Good.

 E-ZEE: Artistic.

 SPARKLEGRRL: Cool.

 F-ZEE: And VERY pretty.

 SPARKLEGRRL: Good? Or bad?

E-ZEE: Bad. According to Flip, L might like her.

SPARKLEGRRL: That stinks. What does K think?

 E-ZEE: Don't know. But L's not the only thing K has 2 worry about.

 SPARKLEGRRL: What else?

 E-ZEE: She's an AMAZING violin player.

 SPARKLEGRRL: BETTER THAN K???!!!

 E-ZEE: Mayb. K's totally going 2 have competition 4 the violin solo in the musical.

 SPARKLEGRRL: OOOOOOH! K must b soooo mad.

 E-ZEE: There's a new boy 2.

 SPARKLEGRRL: Get out!!!

E-ZEE: I know. Crazy, right? Conrad. He's cute . . . at least Chloe thinks so. ☺

 SPARKLEGRRL: Wow! Now u have so many friends I don't even know.

 E-ZEE: And I don't know ANY of ur French friends.

Zee realized that Ally and she were feeling exactly the same way. Major things were happening in Ally's life, and Zee wasn't a part of them. And Ally wasn't there for all of the changes that were happening to Zee. Zee wished the girls could be together again in Brookdale. Then they could just forget about how different their lives had become. But Zee knew that that wasn't going to happen anytime soon, and they'd just have to keep figuring out their friendship over the Internet.

8

Busted!

"Ya'll wanna come over to my house after school today to do homework?" Chloe asked Jasper and Zee as they headed from the cafeteria to science class.

"Sure," Zee said. "I'll call my mom to let her know."

"I can't," Jasper said. "I'm having trouble with one of my scenes with Landon. I'm going to ask him if he wants to help me with it after school today."

"Really?" Zee asked. "You're going to work on the musical with Landon—voluntarily?"

"Don't act so surprised," Jasper said.

"I just didn't think you guys were getting along very well," Zee said.

"I can't let my fellow thespians down," Jasper replied.

"I'm sure you know what that big word means," Chloe said, "but you might want to talk more like a seventh grader so the rest of us can understand you."

"Actors," Jasper said. "I can't let the other actors down. Besides, Mr. P says this performance will be a major part of our grade."

"That's okay," Chloe said. "Zee and I will just have to hang out all by ourselves." She laid the back of her hand across her forehead and swooned. "I hope we can make it."

Zee smiled at Jasper. Maybe she'd only imagined tension between Jasper and Landon.

When the three friends reached the science room, Landon was already sitting on the tall stool beside his lab table. Kathi, his lab partner, was there, too.

"Landon—" Jasper said, walking over to the table. "I had a few ideas about our first scene in Act One. Do you want to work on it with me today after school?"

Landon looked from Jasper to Zee. "I was going to ask Zee if she wants to work on our duet."

"Yes," Zee blurted out. *Oops.* She felt bad about changing plans with Chloe, but she couldn't give up the opportunity to rehearse with Landon. Right?

"I thought you wanted to go over to Chloe's," Jasper said.

"That was before I needed to work on this," Zee explained.

"Well, at least Jasper can come over now," Chloe said as she and Jasper walked to their lab table together.

But Zee thought she heard some sarcasm in Chloe's voice.

Hi, Diary,

I told my teacher I had to go to the bathroom, but I really just needed to talk to you. I have to make it quick, though—since it's not so much fun sitting in the girls' room.

Chloe and Jasper are acting like I chose Landon over them. But I didn't! Landon and I are the LEADS. If we're horrible, the entire musical will be bad.

And when Jasper said he was going to work on the musical, no one cared. But when I said it, it was like I'd committed some major crime. I know I'm right. So why do I feel so crummy?

Zee

Zee hid her diary under her vest and walked out of the bathroom stall.

When Zee got to the music room after school, Landon was already there. *Yay!* Sitting right next to Missy. *Boo!* Had Landon invited the new girl to work with him, too?

"When did you move to Brookdale?" Landon asked Missy.

"Just last week," Missy said. "We moved from South Africa. That's why I started late this year."

"Africa?" Landon looked surprised.

Missy nodded. "My mom was working for Doctors Without Borders."

"Hey, guys!" Zee interrupted, trying to squeeze between Landon's and Missy's desks.

"Oh, hi," Landon answered.

"I didn't know you were staying late, too," Zee said to Missy. She tried to sound casual.

"Mr. P wanted to help me get caught up on the musical, so he asked me to stay after school," Missy explained.

Their teacher entered the room and pointed at Missy. "I'll fill Missy in on the Beans and all the excitement that's in store for her this year"—he moved his finger back and forth from Zee to Landon—"then we'll talk about your big duet. Deal?"

The three students nodded. "Deal," Zee said.

As Missy walked toward Mr. P, Zee turned to Landon. What would they do now?

"Umm . . . do you know what you're going to wear for Friends' Day yet?" Zee asked Landon.

Landon shrugged. "No."

O-*kay*. That didn't exactly get the conversation rolling. Zee searched for something else. "Are you going to hang out with Marcus after we're done?" It was the first thing that popped into her head.

"Marcus is with Conrad." Landon looked at the ground.

"What are they doing?" Zee asked.

"I dunno," Landon said. "They do a lot of stuff together."

"Ummm—" Zee tried to think of something to say. Obviously, she had not picked the best topic to talk about. She felt horrible for Landon. But she was glad she could be there for him. "After we talk to Mr. P, maybe we could keep working on our parts."

"Okay."

At that moment, a man Zee had never seen before appeared in the doorway. He was kind of short, with curly black hair and a smile on his face.

"Dad?" Missy said. "You didn't have to come into the

school to get me. I would have come outside."

Zee hadn't thought it was possible, but she actually felt sorry for this gorgeous, talented, smart girl. It was fine for your parent to show up in your lower school classroom. But upper school? How embarrassing! Zee would hide under a desk if that ever happened to her.

"I wanted to meet your teacher," Mr. Vasi said, holding out his right hand for Mr. P to shake.

"Thanks for taking time out of your schedule to visit," Mr. P said.

Missy's dad nodded. "My pleasure. I'm in between projects now anyway."

"What kind of projects?" Mr. P asked.

"I make documentary films."

Cool beans! Zee thought. *Maybe Mr. Vasi could help shoot the Beans' first video someday!*

"Okay, Daddy, let's go," Missy said, grabbing her father's arm and tugging him out of the room. "I have to get home and start my homework."

Zee watched the two of them leave.

After Zee and Landon talked to Mr. P about their big song, they went outside to practice. The Brookdale Academy campus was covered with thousands of plants and trees native to California. The two of them sat under a willow's drooping branches.

"Maybe we should read through the dialogue you wrote right before the song," Landon suggested.

"That's a good idea," Zee said, handing him part of the script. "We haven't done that together yet."

"Lily starts," Zee said, then took a deep breath. *"Dylan, what are you doing here? My friends will freak out if they see you."*

"I know. The whole football team is trying to keep us apart."

"I'm glad you came."

Landon paused and looked up from his page. "The script says that I should move closer," he said. "Should I do that now?"

"Ummm . . . okay," Zee said. "Then just start with the next line."

As Landon wiggled forward, Zee's heart skipped a beat. *"I could never stay away from you,"* he said. *"I've had a crush on you since we were little kids."*

"Me too." Omigosh! Zee thought. *Did I write that?* The words sounded more like a page out of her diary than fiction.

Embarrassed by the confession she'd written, Zee began giggling. The harder she tried to stop, the worse it got. She covered her mouth and turned her head—just in time to see her mother pull up in her gray Prius. The passenger-side window was down, and Zee noticed that her mother looked upset.

"I expected you to come home after school," Mrs. Carmichael said. *Uh oh.* Zee had forgotten to call. "Why didn't you pick up your Sidekick?"

Zee pulled out her phone. "Sorry," Zee said. "The battery died. I didn't know you were calling."

Zee's mother reached across the front seat and popped open the door. "Get in, please." Then she looked at Landon. "Would you like a ride, Landon?"

"Uh . . . I guess," Landon said. He opened the back door and climbed in.

For a while no one said anything. Mrs. Carmichael gripped the steering wheel so tightly Mackenzie thought she'd squeeze right through it.

"What were you two doing?" Zee's mother finally asked.

"We were working on one of our scenes," Zee told her.

"For the musical?" Mrs. Carmichael asked skeptically. She peered into the rearview mirror to look at Landon. "You guys are taking this so seriously, you'd think you were theater professionals, not twelve-year-olds."

"Actually," Landon began quietly, "I'm thirteen."

Noooooo! Zee telepathically communicated to him—much too late for it to do any good.

"Oh, you're a teenager already," Mrs. Carmichael said.

Please don't embarrass me! Zee silently pleaded with her mother. *I'll do anything. I'll scrub the toilets until I'm forty.*

"Landon, do you think your parents are worried about where you are?" Zee's mom asked. Evidently, a lifetime of clean toilets was not enough for Ginny Carmichael. Zee was humiliated.

"Uh, no," Landon said carefully. "They're at work, and I texted my sister to let her know I was staying after school. I just sent her another text to tell her you're bringing me home."

"That was very responsible of you," Mrs. Carmichael said to Landon, but she was looking at Zee—who slid down in her seat a little and decided to admire the scenery out the window.

"Thanks for the ride," Landon said when they arrived at his house. He hurried to his front door, without looking back. Zee sank in her seat a little more. "Bye, Dylan," she said. "I mean, Landon."

For the rest of the ride home, Zee tried to make her mother forget how upset she was. "I can't believe how much homework I have," she said. "I'm going to be up all night doing it."

"Maybe it's not a good idea to spend so much time with the boys—the Beans, I mean—if you're neglecting your schoolwork," Mrs. Carmichael said.

"But I love music," Zee said. "And besides, there's so much to do before the show. I haven't even started memorizing my lines. If I wait until the last minute, it will be even worse. Plus, there's a lot more script to write. And I have to design the costumes. And compose the music."

"It sounds as though you think you have to do it all yourself."

"That's the thing. Everyone is doing a lot—and there's still probably not enough time to get it all done."

"Hmmmm," Mrs. Carmichael said.

"What?" Zee asked,

"Just thinking."

Uh-oh. That's exactly what Zee was afraid of.

As Mrs. Carmichael pulled into the family's driveway, Zee fished around in her bag for her diary. When she pulled out her binder to see better, Zee's English quiz, with a big red D+, floated to the floor of the car. Zee rushed to pick it up, but it was too late.

"What's that?" Mrs. Carmichael asked, pointing.

"My English quiz," Zee said meekly. "It was really hard."

"Did you study for it?"

"Yes, but I had a lot of other stuff to do that night," Zee explained.

"Maybe you just need help organizing your priorities," Mrs. Carmichael said as she handed Zee the paper.

But Zee knew that her mother would never understand what was really important to her. It was Zee's dream to be a star, and the musical was her opportunity to shine.

* * *

People Who Don't Get It*

Chloe

Jasper

Mom (and probably Dad
        since they're usually a team)

*But I still love them!

People Who Get It**

Mr. P

Ally

Landon

**I'm glad I have them.

Even though Zee knew her mother would probably give birth to a cow if she caught her, Zee decided to check out the Beans' blog. She was working so hard on her parts of the musical, she wanted to see what progress everyone else had made.

Marcus and Conrad had posted a song they'd mixed for the soundtrack! Zee clicked on the clip. An amazing sound streamed through the computer's speakers. "Cool beans!" Zee read Conrad's description of how the boys had gone to the mall and recorded the sounds there. Then they put it all together in the school's music studio.

But as Zee logged off, her excitement faded away. She remembered what Landon had said about how much time Marcus was spending with Conrad. The music was incredible, but would Landon feel left out that Marcus and Conrad had recorded it without him? Zee felt bad for Landon.

9
Mother's Helper

"How was your afternoon, Zee?" Mr. Carmichael asked at dinner that night.

Zee put a forkful of salmon in her mouth and looked at her mother. "Fine?" she said suspiciously, certain her parents had already talked.

"What did you do?"

"I worked really hard on my homework." Zee spoke fast. "For all my subjects—except music. I even did extra credit for English."

"I'm glad that you did your schoolwork," Zee's dad continued. "But I think we need to have a talk."

"About what?" Zee asked.

"Yeah, about what?" Adam chimed in.

Mrs. Carmichael looked at Adam with her this-doesn't-concern-you face, then turned back to Zee.

"It's not a good idea to give all of your attention to one thing."

"You mean, like English?" Zee asked hopefully.

"No, I mean like the musical."

"But I know I want to be a singer. And a songwriter," Zee added. "And Mr. P thinks I'm really good."

"Your dad and I think you're really good, too," Mrs. Carmichael said.

Adam held up his finger, then gulped down a mouthful of barley salad. "For the record, I think you're really good, too."

"Awww . . . thanks!" Zee said, turning to her brother.

Adam pointed back to their parents. "Pay attention."

"You're only twelve," Mrs. Carmichael continued.

"You've got your whole life to become a singer," Zee's dad added.

"Is this about the D plus?" Zee protested. "I *promise* it won't happen again. I can handle all my classes *and* the musical. I can get back on track."

"We're worried about Landon, too," Mrs. Carmichael said.

"What about him?" Zee asked.

"You might be a little too focused on him as well."

"He's my costar!"

"Is that the only reason?"

Adam started making kissing noises, so Zee kicked him under the table.

"Owww!" her brother cried out. "That's the last time I compliment you."

"If you're going to rehearse with Landon," Mrs. Carmichael continued, "it has to be in Mr. P's classroom or here."

Zee's cheeks started to burn. "But—" Zee began.

"We've talked about it and believe it's the best solution," Mr. Carmichael said. "We do realize there's a lot to get done before the show—"

Finally, Zee thought, *they get it.*

"So I'll be helping out in the classroom," Mrs. Carmichael said.

"What?" Zee shouted.

"Sweet!" Adam said. "I should have popped some popcorn for this."

"What do you mean *in* the classroom?" Zee asked.

"You know." Mrs. Carmichael stabbed her salad with her fork. "I'll come and work with the students on whatever needs to be done—building, painting, recording, anything. Even costumes!"

"While I'm there?"

"Yes, of course."

"I don't know if Mr. P will like that." Zee scrambled for an excuse. "He probably doesn't want parents interfering with his class."

"Oh, he loves the idea," Mrs. Carmichael said. "I talked to him about an hour ago."

"You did?"

Mrs. Carmichael nodded enthusiastically, and Zee forced a smile. "Great." She couldn't even look at Adam, who was quietly snickering.

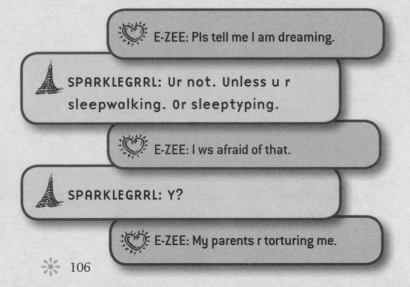

E-ZEE: Pls tell me I am dreaming.

SPARKLEGRRL: Ur not. Unless u r sleepwalking. Or sleeptyping.

E-ZEE: I ws afraid of that.

SPARKLEGRRL: Y?

E-ZEE: My parents r torturing me.

SPARKLEGRRL: ?

 E-ZEE: Mom wants 2 help w the musical!!! In the classroom!!!

 SPARKLEGRRL: OMGYG2BK

 E-ZEE: I wish.

 SPARKLEGRRL: I'm glad mine travel a lot.

 E-ZEE: Now L will never want 2 date me. That'll make my parents happy.

 SPARKLEGRRL: Y?

 E-ZEE: They don't want me near L. They think he's 2 old.

 SPARKLEGRRL: I'm lucky my parents let me c my b/f when I want. 2morrow we r going 2 the Louvre to see the Mona Lisa. J says I remind him of her. ☺

107 ✳

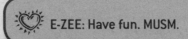
E-ZEE: Have fun. MUSM.

SPARKLEGRRL: <33

The next day in first period, Zee's mother held up two paint samples—one red, one blue. "Which color do you think will look better for the mall sign?" she asked, stepping into the space between Zee and Landon.

"I think the red one," Zee said halfheartedly.

"What about you, Landon?" Mrs. Carmichael asked.

Landon studied the two colors carefully. "I kinda like the blue one."

Kathi looked up from where she and Jasper were working on their own scene nearby. "I agree with Zee," she put in. "The audience will be able to see red better."

"That's true," Mrs. Carmichael said. "Now that that's decided, maybe I can help you and Zee study your lines, Landon."

"Uh . . . I guess," Landon said.

Zee looked from her mother to Kathi and had a horrible realization. Ever since Mr. P had cast the musical, Kathi had been really nice to her. She hadn't acted jealous of her and Landon, or tried to keep them apart, like she usually did. Instead it was Zee's own mom keeping her and Landon apart!

"Where's Marcus?" Chloe asked, looking at the empty seat next to Landon at the lunch table that afternoon.

"He's in the recording studio with Conrad," Jen said in a singsong know-it-all voice.

Landon sank down in his seat a little. Then Missy came over with her lunch tray. "May I sit here?" she asked, pointing to the blank space.

Landon straightened up. "Sure."

Missy sat down and turned to Zee. "You and your mom must be really great friends," she said as she opened her carton of milk.

"Why?" Zee wondered out loud. *Because she practically glued herself to me today?*

"Well, my dad said he wanted to come help out in the classroom, but I told him, 'No way,'" Missy explained. "I'd feel like such a geek having him around."

Chloe jumped in. "Well, Zee's mom is really, really awesome."

"Oh, yeah," Zee agreed. "She's the best."

"So I know you guys really like music. That's pretty obvious. What else do you like to do?" Missy asked, changing the subject. As she spoke, she twisted her long, dark hair around her fingers.

Chloe swallowed a bite of an energy bar. "I play soccer. And Jasper and I are in charge of the campus planting project."

Jasper looked up from his tomato-and-cucumber salad and smiled.

"I like to surf!" Landon joined in.

"That must be why you're so tan," Missy said to him.

"Yeah, you can definitely tell the bennies from the surfers," Landon told her.

"Bennies?"

"Oh, sorry. The tourists. Actually, they even have a name for young surfers—groms."

"Well, I'm not exactly a benny or a grom, but it would be cool to come watch you sometime."

"Awesome!" Landon didn't take his eyes off her.

Missy looked around at the others at the table. "The Beans could have a beach party after."

"I have the perfect new bikini for it," Kathi put in.

That's it? Zee silently asked Kathi. *Aren't you going to give Missy a* hands-off Landon *comment?* For once, Zee wanted Kathi's claws to come out, but it was like she didn't even care!

If Kathi wasn't going to do anything, Zee would have to. She had no choice but to get Landon away from Missy.

"Ummmm . . . Landon?" Zee said. "I just remembered, I want to talk to you about your costumes. I cut out a bunch of pictures from magazines and catalogs, but I left them in my locker. Do you want to come with me and look at them?"

"Do you want me to come, too?" Kathi asked.

Now Kathi wanted to get involved? "No, I can handle it," Zee said.

"But Kathi is working on costumes with you," Jasper pointed out. "I think she should go."

Zee pointed to Kathi's half-eaten lunch. "She shouldn't have to interrupt her lunch."

"No prob," Kathi said. "I'd rather hang out here. I didn't want you to think I was slacking off."

"Your mother would spontaneously combust if she found out you were going off with Landon alone," Chloe whispered.

Zee looked around. "We're not going to be alone. There are a ton of people here."

"You know that's not what she meant," Chloe said.

"You're one of my best friends," Zee whispered. "Aren't you rooting for me and Landon?"

"I'm looking out for you," Chloe said. "And if my best friend is grounded, I won't get to hang out with her."

"I won't get grounded if no one tells my parents." Zee turned away from Chloe. "Come on, Landon," she said.

Zee and Landon headed toward the cafeteria door. Just as she was about to exit, a large body blocked her path. Adam!

"I don't believe this!" Zee slumped forward.

Zee's brother gave her a sly smile. "Nice try," he said.

Zee turned to Landon. "On second thought, I'll show you the costumes in music class tomorrow."

* * *

 E-ZEE: Do ur parents act crazy b/c u have a b/f?

 SPARKLEGRRL: Not really.

 E-ZEE: I wish mine traveled like urs.

 SPARKLEGRRL: No, u don't.

 E-ZEE: U r right, I guess. But I do wish mine didn't have so many rules.

 SPARKLEGRRL: Mine have rules. My nanny is the enforcer. LOL! But she's French, and it's not such a big deal here.

 E-ZEE: I wish I ws French.

 SPARKLEGRRL: THAT I believe. LYLAS.

 E-ZEE: <33

10

Second (-hand) Chances

hile Zee and Chloe finished changing into their gym clothes, Kathi, Jen, and Missy were practicing dance steps for the musical in the locker room. Jen kicked her leg up high, then arched her back.

"Oh, that's so cool," Missy said. "Then we can do this." She reached out, first with her right hand, then with her left.

Zee pulled her gym shirt over her head. "Cool beans!" she said.

"Let's go practice it in the gym," Kathi suggested. "There's more room."

"All right!" Jen bounced excitedly.

"My parents said I can have a sleepover on Friday night," Missy told the others as they headed out of the locker room. "You guys are all invited."

Kathi clapped. "Excellent! I love snooping inside other people's houses."

Chloe turned to her. "You know you said that out loud, don't you?"

"Oh, is there something wrong with that?" Kathi asked.

"My dad said he'd take us all to the International Skate Center," Missy went on.

Tweet! Mr. Lieberman, the gym teacher, blew the whistle hanging from the string around his neck.

"Line up in squads, everyone!" Mr. Lieberman's voice bounced off the gym walls. "Pronto!"

"Oh, joy," Zee said sarcastically. "Gym is starting."

"I guess we'll have to learn the choreography later," Chloe said.

"At the sleepover. I'll email you guys the details," Missy said while they walked across the polished wood floor to their places under the basketball hoop.

"Details for what?" Conrad asked.

"Missy's having a slumber party," Jen explained.

Conrad held out his arms to indicate the other boys. "Are we invited?"

Missy blushed. "My parents would never let me have boys at a sleepover."

"You'll have to have your own party," Jen said.

"That's what I'll do! But, I don't have parties," Conrad said. "I have par-*tays*." Conrad turned to Marcus, Jasper, and Landon. "Are you guys in?" he half shouted, holding up his palms for high fives.

With a running start, Marcus rushed him and slapped Conrad's palm. Then Conrad held his hands in front of Jasper and Landon, who each gave him a high five. When Jasper and Landon faced each other, they let their arms drop and turned away.

* * *

The next day was a big one for Kathi and Missy. They were competing for the violin solo—and Zee knew Kathi was counting on winning. If Missy had never shown up, the part would definitely be Kathi's. But now there were two amazing violinists in the Beans. Kathi had already lost the lead role to Zee, so getting the solo was especially important.

"Kathi and Missy, bring your instruments and come with me, please," Mr. P said after he took roll.

Kathi batted her eyelashes. "Are you going to pick the winner, Mr. P?" she asked.

"No, I've asked Mrs. Zolotow, the choral director, to be the judge," Mr. P explained. "You'll be behind a panel, though, so she won't know who's performing. That will keep it fair."

Kathi looked disappointed, but she and Missy picked up their violins and walked toward their teacher.

"Everyone else should find a partner to work with on the script, songs, or your stage crew committee," Mr. P told the rest of the class. "Mrs. Carmichael is in charge, so please listen to her."

Zee turned around to Landon, who was staring at her mother. "Hey, Landon, do you—" she began.

"Want to work on props with me?" Landon quickly asked Jen.

"Sure," Jen said.

Mom strikes again! Zee told herself, disappointed.

Kathi was the first to return from the audition. "How'd it go?" Zee asked.

"Whatev," Kathi said, putting her violin in its case. "I didn't really care about it. I have all those lines to memorize already." When she turned her face away, Zee was sure she heard a sniffle.

Then Missy walked in with a big smile on her face. Zee couldn't believe Kathi had lost the violin solo. Was her reign finally over?

After school, Zee changed into a pair of shorts and a gray camisole, and laced up her white Converse high-tops. *The perfect costume-hunting outfit!* she thought. She and Kathi were going to the thrift shop to buy costumes for the musical. Zee hopped on her bike and pedaled to Kathi's house.

Zee rang the Barneys' bell, and Kathi answered right away.

"Perfect timing," Kathi said. "My sister was just about to leave. She can drive us to the store now."

"Why don't we just ride bikes?" Zee suggested. "It's really close."

"Can't," Kathi told her.

"Isn't that your bike right there?" Zee said, pointing to a red-and-blue bike she could see inside the open garage.

"Yes, but I'm not supposed to ride it."

"Why do you have it then?"

"'Cause it's the best one available," Kathi said. "But if I ride it, I might ruin it. Then it would just be a used bike."

"Doesn't it bother your parents that they paid for a bike that you never ride?"

"It's their idea," Kathi said. "They like for things to look perfect."

Zee looked at her own bike and thought about all of the bike rides her family took together. She had a memory for every ding and scratch.

"Let's just walk," Zee suggested.

Kathi's phone rang as the girls headed toward the thrift shop. "Hi, Mom," she answered. "No, I didn't get the solo." Zee heard a weird noise come through the phone—like a howl—then words she didn't understand. "I guess Missy just played better," Kathi said. A pause. "I don't know, Mom." Another pause. "Do you really think Mr. P likes her better?" More inaudible squeaking came through Kathi's cell phone. "Well, no, you definitely shouldn't blame me." Kathi listened. "You're right—the audition was fixed."

After Kathi hung up, Zee stayed silent.

"I'm just glad I didn't have to tell my mom to her face," Kathi said. "I so didn't want to see her disappointed look." She furrowed her brows and frowned to mimic her mother.

"I don't think Mr. P would play favorites," Zee said. "Do you?"

"Of course I do!" Kathi said. "But if he did choose a favorite, I'm sure it would be me. That's why I think somehow Missy cheated to get the part."

"How?" Zee asked. Did Kathi think *Zee* cheated to get the lead?

"I don't know how—maybe Mrs. Zolotow was in on it—but Missy's sweet routine is definitely just an act," Kathi said. "No one that pretty needs to be that nice."

Even though Kathi's logic seemed kind of strange, Zee agreed that Missy was a mystery. "We really don't know much about her," Zee said.

"No, we don't," Kathi said. "But I think she's the kind of person who doesn't care who she hurts to get what she wants."

Does Missy want Landon? Zee wondered. Was she going to try to take him away from Zee?

The girls soon arrived at a strip mall that included an antiques store, a framing shop, and a barbershop as well as the thrift shop.

Kathi looked around at the racks of clothes that were crammed with jeans, shirts, jackets, and dresses. "So, what exactly is a thrift shop?" she asked, rushing to the bookcases that lined the sides of the room and were stacked with folded sweaters.

Zee looked at Kathi's orange Gucci stretch jeans and Versace T-shirt. She guessed that the clothes Kathi was wearing cost her at least $500. The sneakers were another $150. She wasn't surprised Kathi didn't know what a thrift shop was.

"It's a place where people donate clothes they don't want anymore. Then the store resells them."

"You mean, it's used stuff—like hand-me-downs?" Kathi crinkled her nose and frowned.

Zee nodded. Kathi rushed away, but instead of going right back out the front door, as Zee expected, she hurried over to a rack of jeans, nearly tripping over a basket of belts that was sitting on the floor.

"Awesome!" Kathi exclaimed. After frantically pushing hangers along the metal bar, she grabbed a pair of jeans and held them up. "I love these. My parents would never let me wear them—but for the musical, I could get away with it." A wild, mischievous smile spread across her face.

"Now all you need is a shirt, and your costume's done," Zee said. "How much are the jeans?"

Kathi checked the tag. "Only a hundred dollars."

"A hundred dollars?" Zee looked for herself. Someone had neatly written $1.00 in blue ink. *Ohmylanta!* Zee silently groaned. "You've definitely never been to a thrift shop. It's only a dollar."

Kathi laughed at her mistake. "Thank goodness you're here to help me with this!" she said, crushing Zee in a hug.

E-ZEE: K strikes again!

SPARKLEGRRL: OMG! What did she do?

E-ZEE: She ws NICE!

SPARKLEGRRL: A trick?

E-ZEE: Nt sure. It doesn't feel fake.

SPARKLEGRRL: Y?

E-ZEE: She hardly notices L anymore—like she doesn't like him.

SPARKLEGRRL: So who does she like?

 E-ZEE: Don't know. Mayb it's nt about boys. Mayb it's b/c she doesn't like Missy.

 SPARKLEGRRL: Jealous?

 E-ZEE: She thinks M can't b trusted.

 SPARKLEGRRL: Y? What did she do?

 E-ZEE: Nothing. Yet.

 SPARKLEGRRL: K's the 1 I don't trust.

It was good to talk to Ally. She knew Kathi as well as Zee did—almost. Still, Zee wasn't sure if Ally was right about Kathi or not.

Hi, Diary,

I'm so confused! Is Missy's sleepover just part of her plan to take over Brookdale Academy? Is helping in the classroom just part of Mom's plan to make sure I never, ever have a boyfriend? Is Kathi really a friend now? With the musical keeping me so busy, I don't have time to figure any of this out.

Maybe if I separate the good stuff from the bad stuff, it will help.

Good Stuff	Bad Stuff
Ally will always be THE BEST bff ever! (I know I totally overreacted about her "being equal." comment.)	Mom doesn't understand what it's like to be 12.
	Still no boyfriend.
I get to spend more time with Landon.	Still no boobs.

Zee looked at her list, wondering where to put Kathi. Kathi could be a lot of fun, but Zee knew that could change faster than she could say, "Who just stuck that knife in my back?"

Then Zee had an idea. She added a third column especially for Kathi.

2 Good 2 B True Stuff
Kathi

✿ 11 ✿
Sleepover Disaster

$\mathcal{Z}$ee shoved a pair of heart-printed pajama pants and a plain red tank top into the overnight bag she was packing for Missy's sleepover. She grabbed a pair of green pants from a hanger. Just before she dropped them into the bag, she stopped herself. *These would be perfect for Friends' Day.* She quickly substituted a shirt and a pair of denim capri pants that Zee had converted from an old pair of jeans by cutting off the bottoms and adding a wide ribbon trim.

"Clothes for tomorrow." Zee began her mental list. "Check.

Toothbrush and toothpaste? Check and check," she said, adding them to the bag. "Oops! I almost forgot the most important thing." She rushed over to her dresser. "Clean underwear. Checkity check check." She pulled the zipper closed on her bag.

Zee and Chloe arrived at the party together and rang the doorbell. Instead of a simple *ding-dong*, the Vasis' doorbell boomed four notes. It sounded as if a bell choir were performing right in the foyer. A woman in a simple black dress and white apron opened the door, then bowed her head slightly.

"Hi," Zee said. "Is Missy here?"

"Right this way, miss," the woman said formally. She led Chloe and Zee into a room with a black grand piano. Heavy red, black, and orange silk curtains hung at the windows, and colorful wool rugs covered the floor. "May I take your bags?" the woman offered.

Zee and Chloe handed theirs to her. "Where are you taking them?" Chloe called out. But the woman just smiled and walked away.

"Great!" Missy's cheerful voice came into the room as she half skipped, half walked toward Zee and Chloe. "Everyone's here." Kathi and Jen followed behind. Then Mr.

Vasi and Missy's younger twin brothers, Zane and Steven, came into view.

"Welcome!" Mr. Vasi said, greeting the girls. "We were just about to show everyone the rest of the house." He began to walk toward the twisting center staircase. The girls walked behind him.

"I'll show you my dad's video studio and screening room later," Missy told Zee and Chloe.

"Where's your mother?" Chloe asked Missy.

"At the hospital," Missy said.

"Is she sick?" Zee asked.

Missy giggled. "No, she's a doctor. She got called into emergency surgery today and she's not home yet. Sometimes brain surgery lasts ten hours."

"*Brain* surgery? Get out!" Chloe said. "I thought that was just an expression. You know, 'It's not brain surgery.'"

"Someone's got to do it," Missy said, "like my mom. I'll show you where she keeps the jars with brains in them."

Zee's stomach flip-flopped. "Really?" she asked.

"No." Missy tossed her head back and laughed. The others joined in. *Had Missy purposely embarrassed her?* Zee wondered.

Upstairs, Missy's bedroom was as fancy as the rest of

the house. She had a plasma HDTV on the wall above her dresser. A desktop computer *and* the latest Mac laptop sat on her desk. Strings of beads hung around Missy's canopy bed. And a large wall hanging embroidered with huts, animals, people, and cacti decorated a wall.

"This room is so awesome!" Chloe said. She looked at the blue, orange, red, and yellow wire-and-bead bird statues that stood on top of Missy's dresser. "Where did you get these?"

"I brought them back from South Africa," Missy said. "One of the women in the village where we lived used to sell them by the side of the road. That's how a lot of the people made money. I bought one nearly every week. They only cost about a dollar, but that was a lot of money to the people who came to my mother's clinic."

"You're so lucky to have lived somewhere with such cool crafts," Chloe told Missy. "Isn't she, Zee?"

"Yeah," said Zee. Even though Missy's room definitely qualified as fantabsome, and she'd love to be able to make crafts like Missy's one day, for some reason Zee couldn't bring herself to tell Missy that.

"It must have been so amazing to live in Africa," Chloe went on. "Did you see any elephants?"

"Lots," Missy told her. "In the Addo Elephant National Park."

"A whole park for elephants?"

"There's also a park for zebras—the Mountain Zebra National Park."

"Get out!" Chloe said, her mouth opening wide.

While everyone else was listening and touring Missy's cavernous closet—with an entire alcove for shoes—Kathi changed into her new thrift-shop jeans.

"Aaaaah!" Jen was the first to see her best friend. Chloe gasped out loud, and Missy just looked confused by all the excitement. Zee couldn't believe how easily Kathi made a $1.00 pair of ripped jeans look like Armanis.

"Where did you get those?" Jen asked Kathi.

"They're part of her costume," Zee volunteered.

"But I love them so much, I'm going to wear them to the International Skate Center tonight!" Kathi explained.

"Did you get them on Rodeo Drive, in New York City, or in Paris?" Jen rattled off Kathi's favorite shopping spots.

"Actually, they're from Brookdale Thrift Shop," Kathi said. "Zee and I went together."

Jen looked like she would faint right there, and

Zee wondered if it was because Kathi was wearing someone else's old clothes or because Kathi and Zee were bonding.

"You know you can't do it. You'll make a mistake." The Beans girls circled the ISC roller rink in a group, singing the chorus to one of the songs Mr. P had helped Kathi write. *"'Cause love can be hard, and you've got just one take."*

"Then comes the part where Conrad raps while we dance," Kathi said.

"Oh, my gosh!" Jen said. "He's so good."

"Ooooooh!" Kathi teased, and the other girls joined in.

"I don't like him like that," Jen protested. "I just think he's a good rapper."

Out of nowhere, a body whizzed by, so close it nearly knocked all of them down like a row of dominoes. Conrad! And following close behind him were Landon and Marcus.

Chloe turned around. "Is Jasper here, too?"

"He's over there!" Zee said, pointing. A few feet back, Jasper slowly skated toward the group. He couldn't stop his feet from rolling in opposite directions.

Zee and Chloe waited for their friend. When he finally caught up, Zee grabbed one of his arms while Chloe held on to the other. The girls held him up and dragged him along. "I thought this was just going to be girls' night," Chloe said to Jasper. "Did you know the guys were coming here?"

"I think not," Jasper said. "We were all going to go bowling. When I mentioned to Conrad that you guys would be here, he decided he wanted the lads to come, too."

Ahead, Zee saw Landon grab Missy to keep her from falling. Without thinking, Zee immediately let go of Jasper to try to hurry to Landon and Missy. But Jasper lost his balance without Zee's support.

"Criiiiiikey!" Jasper cried.

"Zee! Help!" Chloe held his arm tight and began to zigzag awkwardly to keep both of them standing.

"Oops!" Zee said, grabbing Jasper's arm, which was flailing off to the side.

When the girls managed to steady Jasper, Zee told him, "Maybe you could sort of hang out near the side for a while—until you get used to the skates."

"Yes, I suppose I could use a rest," Jasper agreed.

As Zee and Chloe guided their friend to safety, Zee watched the others. Kathi, Jen, and Missy whizzed around in a group. Conrad, Marcus, and Landon stuck together, too—except each time they passed the girls, Conrad pretended to try to ram into them. Kathi and Jen always managed to steer out of the way, but he surprised Missy each time, and she wobbled. While Conrad and Marcus raced off, Landon steadied her before catching up with the others.

"I need to get over there," Zee said, although she'd only meant to think it.

"Go on, then," Jasper said. "Both of you."

"Are you sure?" Chloe asked.

"Of course, I am. Frankly, it was getting quite embarrassing being dragged along."

"Let's go," Zee said, looking at Chloe and gliding into the crowd.

"Look out!" Chloe warned.

Zee turned just in time to see Conrad heading straight for her. "Oh, no!" Missy called. Zee swerved out of Conrad's way, but Missy grabbed her arm anyway. Down Zee went—right on her butt.

Conrad raised his arms in the air. "That wasn't my fault. I didn't even touch her."

"Oh, I'm so sorry," Missy apologized to Zee. She reached out her hand to help Zee up. But when Zee took it and began to stand, she just landed on the floor again. Missy let go to keep from falling, too.

"Ohmylanta!" Zee was glad she'd worn a pair of cropped leggings with her short flared skirt. She didn't need the entire ISC to know she was wearing her "Wednesday" underwear on Friday.

Other skaters began to gawk.

"Here!" Missy held out both palms to Zee. "Maybe if you use both hands."

"No, I've got it!" Dodging other skaters, Zee crawled on her hands and knees to the side, right next to where Jasper was still standing. He helped her up.

When Zee looked up, Landon was headed right for her. *Please, please, please*, she silently begged. *Please tell me Landon didn't see that*

whole humiliating scene. "Hi," Zee said when he reached her.

"Are you okay?" Landon asked. "I saw what happened."

"It figures," Zee said.

"What does?" Landon asked.

"Oh, nothing." By now, the rest of the Beans had come over to make sure she was all right. "I think I just need a break."

"Me too," Missy agreed. "Let's go get some pizza."

The girls left to return their skates and get dinner while the boys headed to the arcade.

"It feels so strange to start at a new school so late in the year," Missy said once the girls sat down.

"But thanks to you, I'm not the new girl anymore," Chloe pointed out.

"*You* were the new girl?" Missy sounded surprised. "You look like you've been going to Brookdale forever."

"I moved here from Atlanta over the summer."

"That explains your accent," Missy said. "It's really cute."

"It's just normal to me," Chloe said. "Nothing special."

"What's it like living in the South?" Missy asked her.

Chloe shook her head slightly. "Normal, I guess—like here."

"Really?" Missy asked. "It must be totally different."

"It's not," Chloe told her. Zee detected a not-very-happy tone in Chloe's voice—the same one she used with Kathi sometimes.

If Missy heard it, she didn't let on. Instead she leaned forward and said, "You guys need to tell me who's hot and who's not."

"You can't tell?" Zee asked.

Missy shrugged. "Well, all the guys are cute. I just don't want to have a crush, then find out he's a nose picker."

The table broke out in laughter. Even Chloe joined in.

Kathi sighed. "Well, if you're worried about immature boys, I would avoid all of the students."

"Huh?" Zee said. "Then who's left?"

"The teachers, of course."

"I'm afraid to ask who," Chloe said.

"Whatev," Kathi said. "If you don't want to know . . ."

"We do!" all the girls shouted at once.

"You have to tell us." Missy sounded desperate.

Kathi looked off to each side, then behind her to make

sure the coast was clear. "I think Mr. P is cute."

"Ooooooooh!" the girls groaned.

"He's so old," Jen said. "He must be thirty!"

"The word is *mature*," Kathi corrected her.

Mr. P! That explains Kathi's total lack of interest in Landon, Zee thought.

"Well, I think Marcus is a total cutie!" Chloe spilled, giggling excitedly.

Again the whole table erupted. Even though Chloe had never actually confessed her crush on Marcus to Zee, Zee had figured it out a while ago.

"Marcus?" Jen said indignantly. "You're not exactly his type." It was no secret to most of the group that Jen had a crush on Marcus, too.

Chloe stopped laughing. "What's his type?"

"Someone more feminine."

"Pull-ease—"

"Who do you like, Missy?" Zee cut her off. The girls couldn't fight, or they wouldn't be able to work together on the musical. Plus, this was the perfect opportunity to find out if Missy liked Landon. Zee took a long drink of soda so she wouldn't look too anxious.

"I thought it was obvious," Missy said. "Jasper."

Soda shot across the table before Zee could stop it.

"You like Jasper?" Chloe asked.

"Yeah." Missy got a worried look on her face. "You're just friends, right?"

Chloe nodded. "Uh-huh." She turned to Zee and bit her lower lip.

"What?" Zee said.

"You might want to wipe off your shirt," Chloe said, handing her a napkin.

Zee took it and dabbed at the soda droplets. "Uh . . . yeah . . . Jasper's a really great guy," she said.

"Do you know if he likes anyone?" Missy said.

"He hasn't said anything to me," Zee told her.

Zee was feeling kind of weird. But why? She was definitely happy that Missy didn't like Landon that way, so what was bothering her? *Am I jealous that Missy has a crush on Jasper?*

"These jeans aren't the only cool costumes Zee and I found at the thrift shop," Kathi said, changing the subject.

Zee was happy to move on. "Yeah, Kathi and I were thinking that she and I could wear hoodies and everyone else would have cool T-shirts in the same color."

"We'll do something similar for the boys, too," Kathi added.

"That's cute," Missy said. "But don't you think that's

139

done too much? At my old school, we put on a play, and everyone put together their own costume."

"But Mr. P likes our ideas," Zee said defensively.

"You could suggest my way to him," Missy said.

"What do you think, Zee?" Kathi asked. "Should we ask Mr. P if everyone could create their own costume?"

"No!" Zee said loudly. "Everyone has a job. Ours is costumes."

"You can still be in charge of coordinating everything," Jen suggested.

"That wouldn't be very interesting," Chloe said, looking angrily at Jen. "Besides, no one is butting into anyone else's job."

"That's right!" Zee said. "Because Kathi and I are doing them. No matter what!" First Landon, then Jasper . . . and now costumes. Was Missy going to take *everything* from Zee? "I'm leaving!"

"I'm outta here, too," Chloe said, glaring at Jen.

The girls got up and walked away from the group.

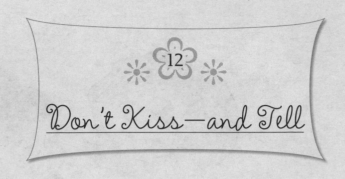

12

Don't Kiss—and Tell

"Now what do we do?" Zee looked around the noisy ISC. She was so upset, the strobing lights and loud music made thinking hard.

Chloe planted her fist on her hip. "I'd like to go back and give them a piece of my mind."

"I think you already did," Zee told her.

"Well, I don't feel like skating anymore. And we can't go to Missy's house now," Chloe said, taking her phone out of her pocket. "I guess I should call my parents to come get us."

Zee suddenly had an idea. "Wait!" she said. "You don't want to bother your parents in the middle of their dinner." Zee felt horrible, but she knew who could make her feel better. Landon.

Chloe slipped her phone back in her pocket. "You're probably right. What now?"

Zee peeked into the arcade. Conrad and Marcus were playing a video game. Jasper sat at a table reading a book. Landon was watching cartoons on the TV in the corner of the room.

"Can you hang out with Jasper while I talk to Landon for a minute?" Zee asked.

"But you're not supposed to be alone with Landon," Chloe told her.

"I'm not breaking my parents' rule at all. You'll be right there with me," Zee pointed out.

"That's true," Chloe agreed. "Okay, I'll do it. I'd rather be with Jasper than those girls anyway."

"Thanks!" Zee didn't know what exactly she was going to say to Landon, so she was a little nervous. She walked to the corner of the room and sat down next to him.

"Hi," he said, surprised.

"You looked kind of lonely sitting here all by yourself," Zee said.

"What?" Landon said, leaning closer.

"How's the party?" Zee tried again.

"I'm not really having fun," Landon said.

Nearby an air hockey puck clacked against the sides of the table, and a group of boys playing foosball shouted.

"It's kind of noisy here," Zee said. "Do you want to go somewhere quieter?"

"Okay. Sure." Together Zee and Landon walked out of the arcade, right past Chloe and Jasper, who were playing Ping-Pong and didn't see them leaving. As soon as they passed through the door, it got quieter. Missy, Jen, and Kathi were still sitting at the table in a huddle. *Gossiping about* me, *probably*, Zee figured.

"Why don't we go outside?" Zee suggested. "I'm done skating anyway."

"Sure," Landon said.

They headed out the front door. Suddenly surrounded by quiet, Zee breathed a sigh of relief. Now she could think more clearly. "We can sit on that bench," she said, pointing to a spot slightly around the corner of the building.

Landon and Zee sat down. "So why aren't you hanging

out with the girls?" he asked.

"We had a fight," Zee said.

"No way! About what?"

"Well, mostly about the costumes," Zee told him.

"Really?" Landon turned to face Zee. "With Kathi?"

"No, she's being cool about it," Zee explained. "But Missy just wants us to do it her way."

"Missy? I didn't know she was like that."

"Well, she is."

Landon scooted closer to Zee. "But it's your job."

"I know," Zee said. "But it's not only her. Everyone wants to tell me what to do."

"Like who?"

"My parents. And my brother." Zee sniffled. She could feel tears puddling in her eyes.

"What are they saying to you?" Landon asked.

"Being a singer is my dream, but they're always telling me it's not as important as other things."

"Yeah, your mom can be pretty intense," Landon agreed.

Tears rolled down Zee's cheeks. "Except for you, no one thinks the musical is as important as I do. Even Chloe and Jasper don't get it. I feel so lonely."

"I know what you mean—you know, when your best

friends aren't there for you." Landon put his arms around Zee. A hug was just what she needed.

Zee looked into his blue eyes. Her heart pounded as they moved closer to her face. Before she knew it, his lips were nearly touching hers.

"There you are, Zee!" Chloe said, coming around the corner.

"With Landon!" Jasper said.

Wiping her tears, Zee quickly stood as Landon slid back to the other end of the bench. "Chlasper and Joey!" Zee shouted. "I mean, Jaspy . . . uh . . . Chlosper. I mean, you surprised me."

"I didn't know where you were," Chloe said.

"And I didn't know where Landon was. Nobody did," Jasper added. "It wasn't very polite of you to leave Conrad's party without telling him."

"It wasn't Landon's fault. I was really upset, and he was just helping me," Zee defended him. "We lost track of time." When she looked over Chloe's shoulder, she realized that she was definitely going to need to defend herself, too. "Ohmylanta! My parents!" Zee said. "What are they doing here?"

J.P. and Ginny Carmichael were walking across the parking lot toward the group, and judging by the looks on their faces, they weren't happy.

"When I couldn't find you, I got desperate," Chloe

explained. "I asked Missy if she had seen you. We were worried, so she called her father." She bit her lip and looked at Zee's parents, who were getting closer. "I guess he called your parents." Chloe handed Zee her purse. "You left this at the table."

Zee rolled her eyes to keep from crying again. She knew she was in big trouble. She never imagined her first kiss would be such a disaster. In fact, it was such a huge disaster that it wasn't even a kiss!

Zee waved to her friends and started walking toward her parents. "I'll see you when—I mean, *if*—I get out of prison."

E-ZEE: OMG!!!!!

SPARKLEGRRL: ?

E-ZEE: L almost kissed me!!!

SPARKLEGRRL: !!! 411 pls.

E-ZEE: The SWAT team came & stopped us.

SPARKLEGRRL: Ur parents?

 E-ZEE: C & J.

 SPARKLEGRRL: R u kidding? They r ur friends.

 E-ZEE: NK. I am grounded 4 2 days. This is my last IM session b4 I go behind bars. But it was worth it. At least I know L likes me!

 SPARKLEGRRL: I'm so jealous. I haven't even kissed my b/f.

 E-ZEE: Really????

 SPARKLEGRRL: I've been practicing.

 E-ZEE: ON WHO?!?!?

 SPARKLEGRRL: LOL! On an apple. I put lipstick on 1st, so I can c if I am doing it right.

E-ZEE: R U?

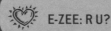 SPARKLEGRRL: I hope so!

 E-ZEE: The Beans still have A BIG prob. No1 is talking.

Zee filled Ally in on the fight.

 SPARKLEGRRL: That is a prob. I c y u r upset, but y not just apologize?

 E-ZEE: 4 what?

 SPARKLEGRRL: Tell thm u want 2 hear their ideas. But u & K will make final decisions. U cld have another party. A costume party 2 plan costumes.

 E-ZEE: WFM! Thx!

 SPARKLEGRRL: NP. GTR. Dad and I r going 2 le marché aux puces de Saint-Ouen.

E-ZEE: ????

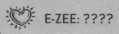 SPARKLEGRRL: Paris flea market. Lots of cool vintage clothes.

 E-ZEE: Like the thrift shop!

 SPARKLEGRRL: Actually, waaay better. Bye!

Zee reread the IM. It was totally cool of Ally to help her out with her problem, but her comment about the thrift shop stung. Did she mean to make Zee feel so bad? Zee thought she'd always be able to count on Ally, but she desperately wished they could hang out together in person. Too much was getting lost over IMs and email. She needed Ally here.

13

Friends? Day

Terms of My House Arrest

1. No leaving the house (of course).
2. No visitors.
3. No computer—unless it's for homework, but even then I have to do it
   where the warden can monitor me.
4. No texting and no phone calls.
   (No kidding—I'm not allowed to
   communicate with my buds.)

   Since my punishment is just for this weekend,
Mom and Dad said I could have my costume party
next weekend.
5. No biggie!

                                        Zee

* * *

With nothing else to do, Zee sat next to her father, thinking about her latest problem. *How am I going to invite everyone to my party if I can't tell them about it?* Zee felt awful about the fight and wanted to make up with all the girls as soon as possible.

Mr. Carmichael tossed an unopened envelope into the kitchen recycling bin. "Junk," he said. "Junk. Junk." He added a catalog to the pile.

"That's it!" Zee exclaimed.

"What's it?" her father asked.

"I'll make homemade invitations for my party today," she explained, picking up the catalog and a magazine that had gotten buried. "I'll cut out pictures and make funny captions."

"I thought you said you already had plans today. I believe your exact words were, 'shrivel up and die of boredom.'"

"Plans change, you know."

"Flexibility is a fine quality to have."

"Later, dude!" Zee stood up and headed to her bedroom. She pulled a basket full of markers, paper, scissors, and glue sticks from under her bed. "This might actually be fun."

Zee grabbed her iPod, which had somehow stayed off the forbidden list, and stuck it into the docking station.

153

Then she turned up the volume and began cutting, folding, and gluing.

Hmmm. Now the hard part—what to say. These had to be invitations *and* apologies, all in one. "Roses are red/ violets are blue," she recited. "I'll admit I was wrong/if you do, too." *Just kidding.*

Zee put her pen to the first card. "I was a jerk/I made a mistake./So let's give this scene/a second take." Zee quickly scribbled down the verse, then kept writing. "Come to my house./We'll all play a part./Wear a wild costume./This is sealed with a—" She glued a pink heart at the end of the final line.

Zee made a card for everyone, then stared at the stack. How would she deliver them since she wasn't allowed to contact anyone? When she heard Adam's feet pounding down the stairs, she had an idea. She followed him into the kitchen. Dressed in his tennis clothes, he was on his way out the door.

"While you're out, can you deliver these to my friends' houses? It's really important." Zee held the stack of cards out in front of him.

Adam stared at the stack. "Are you kidding?"

"No." Zee shook her head.

"Funny, that's what I was going to say." Adam grabbed his tennis racket from the counter and stepped outside. "Bye-onara."

Zee sighed and wondered what she was going to do. Then she remembered the person who might want to patch things up with the group as much as she did: Chloe. Zee found her father and put her arm around his shoulders. "Hello, Daddy."

"What do you want, Zee?" he asked suspiciously.

"I'm going to try not to be offended by your implication."

"And then will you tell me what you're after?"

"Yes, I will. I was wondering if I could make one teensy-weensy phone call to Chloe—" Zee began. Her father's eyes grew wide. "Keeping in mind that she's the one who was looking out for me the other night *and* I need her help to

155 ✳

tell my friends I'm sorry." She handed her dad an invitation. "I want her to deliver these."

Mr. Carmichael read the card. "Just *one* phone call?" he asked.

Zee made an X across her chest. "I promise."

"Well, okay."

"Cool beans!" Zee threw her arms around her dad's neck. "You're fantabsome."

"Is that a compliment?"

"The best!"

As Zee raced out of the room, her dad shouted out, "One phone call!"

"Got it!" Zee told him. "Like a prisoner."

When Zee called, Chloe was heading to her soccer game. "I'll stop at your house on my way home and pick them up," she promised.

Zee reached into the bottom of her book bag to get a pen so she could address the invitations. No pen. She pulled out her binder and textbooks, then looked at the green flier on top. Friends' Day! Zee had completely forgotten.

"Cool beans!" Zee mumbled to herself. "The invitations will arrive just in time for me to actually have my friends back for Friends' Day!"

Tap, tap.

"Come in!" Zee called out.

Mrs. Carmichael opened the door slightly, then pushed her head through the crack. "How's it going?"

"Fine," Zee told her. "I'm trying to figure out if I should wear my green high-top Converses on Monday—or if that'll look too much like a string bean."

Mrs. Carmichael pointed to the mess of craft supplies spread out on the floor. "How about cleaning that up while you think?"

"Okay." Zee got down on her hands and knees to organize the chaos as her mother shut her bedroom door again. She looked at her computer and wondered how many emails she hadn't been allowed to read. Mostly, she wondered how many Landon had sent and what they said. She knew she wouldn't be able to find out until the weekend was over. After all, if her parents—or Adam—caught her, a double grounding would only make matters worse.

Hi, Diary,
You're all I have left.

I'm so confused! What does a kiss even mean? You know, Ally has never kissed her b/f, but she knows he likes her. I almost did kiss Landon, but I have NO IDEA if he likes me. Did he just feel sorry for me? Does he know I like him?

Zee looked at the last question. That was it! Maybe he was just as confused as Zee. She needed a way to let Landon know she liked him. She looked at the art supplies lying all over the floor and decided what to do.

I'll make Landon a Friends' (wink, wink) Day card. That should give him a clue.

Zee

(Just?) Friends' Day

Ally,

Did u miss me? I FINALLY got my computer and phone back this AM. I had A TON of messages. U were so right about the costume party. Every1 is completely into it—and no1 is mad at me anymore. THANKS!!

Unfortunately, there were 0 messages from Landon. I'm sure my parents completely freaked him out. The Friends' Day card I made 4 him is

Earth to LANDON

so cool. Of course, it's really a *More Than Friends*
Day card. I cut out a picture of a woman talking
on the telephone, but I glued a globe over her
face. Then drew a voice bubble that said, "Earth to
Landon." LOL!
WB when u get this!
Zee

Zee turned the dial on her combination lock, then jerked
it open. She checked herself in the mirror that hung inside
her locker and adjusted the light blue scarf around her neck
that highlighted her green sweater perfectly. A note flut-
tered from the shelf to the floor. She picked it up.

"What's that?" Chloe asked. She'd worn an olive-green
tank top with a light green long-sleeved shirt and camou-
flage capris.

"I don't know," Zee said.

"What's it say?"

The outside was decorated with green smiley stickers.
Zee opened it up and read, "'You're a great friend! Happy
Friends' Day! (Think green.)'"

"Who's it from?" Chloe wondered out loud.

"It just says, 'a secret admirer.'" A smile spread across
Zee's face. "But I know who that is."

Chloe grinned, too. "You do?"

"Landon, of course!"

Chloe's smile disappeared. "Why do you think it's Landon?"

"Because he wants me to know he likes me," Zee said as she started walking to class.

Chloe hurried to catch up with her. "Maybe it's someone else—who just wants to be sure you like him first before he tells you."

"That doesn't make sense," Zee countered. "How can he find out if I like him if I don't know who he is?"

"I guess he didn't think of that," Chloe said quietly.

"Huh?"

"Nothing."

When the girls turned the corner, Jasper was heading in their direction. He was wearing his khaki dress pants with a green collared shirt and his blue uniform jacket. He also had on his new sneakers.

"You look happy," Jasper said to Zee, turning to walk with her and Chloe.

"I am," Zee told him. "I got a Friends' Day card in my locker."

"That's ace. Do you know who delivered it?"

"Umm . . . yeah." Zee hurried her pace, eager to get to

first period—and Landon.

When the three friends arrived in class, Landon hadn't gotten there yet. But Kathi zipped across the room as soon as she saw Zee. She was juggling an armful of cards and flowers.

"Who gave you all that?" Zee asked.

"A bunch of guys," Kathi said without much interest. "Mostly eighth graders. You want one?"

"No, thanks," Zee said, holding her own card tight to her chest.

"This is for you." Kathi handed Zee a small cardboard box, then said, "Happy Friends' Day!"

"Thanks," Zee said, lifting the lid. Inside was a thin silver necklace chain with a flower pendant. It wasn't Zee's style, but it was nice of Kathi to think of her.

"My aunt gave it to me for my birthday," Kathi explained. "I didn't like it, so I thought you would—since I know you like used stuff."

Even when she was being nice, Kathi was Kathi. It was hard for her not to think about herself first. "It's pretty," Zee said. "Thanks."

"Hey, Zee!" Chloe said, placing the bow on her cello strings. "Listen to what Jasper and I wrote for the musical this weekend." As she started to play, Jasper joined in on his bass.

Zee tried to listen, but she kept looking at the door. *When is Landon going to get here?* she wondered.

Suddenly, the music stopped. "That's all we have so far."

"That was really good," Zee said.

"Did you really li—" Jasper began.

At that moment, Landon walked into the room. Zee grabbed the card she'd made for him and hopped out of her chair.

Chloe grabbed Zee's arm. "Where are you going?" she asked.

"To thank Landon for his card."

"Why?" Chloe's voice sounded panicked now.

"Because it's polite."

"Ummm . . . ummm . . ." Chloe desperately searched for words. "The card said it was from a secret admirer. Maybe he wants it to stay a secret."

"That sounds exactly right!" Jasper chimed in.

"If he wanted that, he wouldn't have made it so obvious." Zee shook her head. "You guys are just worried about my mom. Don't—I'm not breaking any rules."

"That's not it." Jasper stood up next to Zee. "Maybe he's shy. You don't want to embarrass him."

"If anyone is shy, it's you," Zee told Jasper and patted him on the back. She turned away and rushed over to Landon. "I got it!" she said to Landon.

"Got what?" Landon asked. His face was blank.

"The card."

"What card?"

Zee's heart dropped. Could she have been wrong about Landon? "You have no idea what I'm talking about, do you?" she asked.

Landon shook his head. Zee hid the card she had made him behind her back and slunk away to her seat.

"What happened?" Chloe asked.

"I'm not sure," Zee said. "But I don't think Landon is my secret admirer."

"Do you have any other ideas who it might be from?" Jasper asked.

"No," Zee said, looking absentmindedly back at Landon.

By the time Zee turned around, Marcus had appeared next to Chloe. "For you!" he said, and with a flourish handed her a rose. Chloe blushed and looked as if she might melt into a puddle right there. After a squeaky "Thank you," she was speechless.

Behind Marcus's back, Zee gave her friend a thumbs-up.

Then Marcus moved down the aisle where Jen and

Kathi were sitting. "For you," he said. "And you." He gave each girl a rose. Jen smirked and looked at Chloe.

Next Marcus circled around to Missy, then back to Zee, delivering his last two roses. "Sorry, guys," he said to the boys. "None for you. Please don't be *green* with envy."

"Darn!" Conrad said, snapping his fingers. "I wanted a pretty flower, too." The boys laughed loudly.

Zee was relieved that everyone was watching the boys, because Chloe seemed embarrassed. She'd obviously thought Marcus had gotten a rose especially for her.

But when Chloe saw Zee looking at her, she whispered, "Well, at least we know Marcus isn't your secret admirer."

Zee giggled and glanced over at Landon.

When Zee arrived in French class, Jen was resting her head in her arms on top of her desk. Zee slid into the chair next to her. "What's up?"

Jen didn't bother to lift her head. "I can't decide which I

hate more—Valentine's Day or Friends' Day," she said. "It's just another day of watching Kathi get all the attention."

"Tell me about it," Zee agreed. "I think Friends' Day is supposed to be more about friend-friends than girlfriends and boyfriends."

"I guess that's the problem. I've got enough buddies." Jen sat up. "I saw what happened with Landon."

"I didn't know my humiliation was so obvious."

"Don't worry about it. Probably no one else noticed," Jen reassured her. "Besides, guys are weird."

"You mean . . . like Marcus?" Zee asked.

"Yeah—and whoever gave you that card."

"You know about the card I got?"

"I heard you talking to Landon. Why doesn't the real guy just confess?"

A bell rang overhead to mark the start of the period. A moment later, Marcus ran across the room, then suddenly put on the brakes. He sat in the desk in front of Jen. "We can start now," he joked. "I'm here!"

Jen rolled her eyes and sighed. Zee knew how she felt. Would they ever figure guys out?

* * *

Who Could My Secret Admirer Be?

Suspect	Motive	Degree of Suspicion *on a scale of 1–5
Marcus	He goofs around a lot, so maybe he's just playing a joke.	3
Conrad	He's new—and might be shier than he seems.	2
Adam	He never passes up the opportunity to play a trick.	4
Landon	He just chickened out. (Please, please let it be him!!)	5

As Zee locked her diary, she got a text from Jasper

>Coming 2 the Amer football game w C & me 2nite?

Zee really needed to finish her final scene *and* write her solo song, but for once she was actually glad to be too busy for her friends. She was still embarrassed and confused about what had happened with Landon that morning, and she wasn't ready to talk with Jasper and Chloe.

>No. 2 bz.

15

Telling Secrets

 E-ZEE: OMG! I'm sooooo glad this week is over.

 SPARKLEGRRL: Y?

 E-ZEE: We have been rehearsing like crazy. It's exhausting!

 SPARKLEGRRL: Ooooooh! Lots of time w L!

 E-ZEE: He still won't look @ me. (Thx, Mom.)

SPARKLEGRRL: R u sure it's totally her fault? What about the weird Friends' Day thing?

 E-ZEE: Don't remind me. Landon's even totally awkward when we r rehearsing— & he's supposed 2 b in character.

 SPARKLEGRRL: U have 2 talk 2 him.

 E-ZEE: I know. But I don't know what 2 say.

 SPARKLEGRRL: U'll figure it out.

 E-ZEE: I hope so. Plus, the costume party is 2nite. I hope I don't fall asleep b4 every1 gets here!

 SPARKLEGRRL: Then it would really b a sleepover.

 E-ZEE: LOL!

"Oooooh! I love this part!" Zee ran over to her computer and turned the speakers up full blast. Zee and Chloe bopped, bounced, and sang along to the music at the top of their lungs. Chloe and Jasper had written this song, then Conrad and Marcus had mixed the music and uploaded it on to the Beans' blog. The whole cast would sing it live at the performance.

Chloe held a braid of white, blue, and yellow streamers in her hand. She and Zee were decorating Zee's bedroom for the costume party. "How are we going to hang these up?" Chloe asked. "We're not tall enough."

"Maybe Adam could help us," Zee explained. "He's freakishly tall."

"He's not a freak," Chloe said, blushing.

"You don't know him like I do," Zee said. She picked up her Sidekick and called Adam on his cell phone in his room.

"Speak to me," Adam said, picking up the phone.

"Can you help us?" Zee asked.

"What do I get?" Adam answered.

"The reward of knowing you did a good deed."

"So . . . you're saying you'll owe me?"

"Fine," Zee said, pushing the button to end the call.

"Is he coming?" Chloe asked, her voice wobbling a little.

"Yes."

"Oh, my gosh!" Chloe panicked. "I gotta make sure my hair looks okay." She tossed the streamer into the air and hurried into the bathroom off Zee's bedroom.

"Don't worry about it. He hasn't brushed his hair in a week," Zee called out to her. Then she added, "It's probably been that long since he washed it, too."

Chloe was silent the entire time Adam was in the room. She just stared at him—unless he faced her, then she quickly looked away.

After Adam left, Zee pointed to Chloe's shirt and asked, "Is that drool?"

"Not hardly," Chloe said. "I accidentally splashed myself in the bathroom."

"If you say so . . . ," Zee said and laughed. "We should put on our costumes now before everyone else gets here."

Chloe changed into a soccer uniform and tucked a ball under her arm. "This is what I wore for my old team in Atlanta."

Zee grabbed a huge yellow T-shirt that she'd decorated with horizontal black stripes. She pulled it on over black leggings. "Can you help me stuff these old towels in my shirt?" she asked Chloe.

"What are you?" Chloe asked.

"You'll see."

When the girls were done, Zee said, "Buzzzzz," then slipped a black plastic hairband over her short red hair. Two giant springs, each with a black ball at the end, swung in the air and knocked into the other.

"Oh, I get it!" Chloe exclaimed. "You're a bee."

"Yup. My dad suggested it, because I've been so bee-Zee lately."

The doorbell rang, and Chloe and Zee hurried to answer it.

"Peace," Kathi said and held up two fingers when Zee

opened the door. Her straight brown hair was parted in the middle and fell over each eye. In addition to a tie-dye T-shirt, she wore her thrift-store blue jeans. "My mother almost went gray when she saw me, but what could she do? It's just a costume, right?"

"I don't know, Kathi," Zee teased. "I think those jeans are now officially part of your wardrobe, since you wear them every chance you get."

Kathi giggled. "I can't help it, considering how good I look in them."

Jen followed Kathi through the door. She had on black glasses that slid down her nose and a red-and-white-striped shirt that she had buttoned to the top. Her pants were belted up high as if they were supporting her boobs. "I'm a nerd," Jen snorted. "Do you want me to fix your computer?"

All of the girls burst into hysterical laughter. Then Jen moved to the side so Zee could see Missy.

"Wow!" Zee was stunned. Missy wore a beautiful plum-colored sari with a green-and-gold border.

"Are you Indian?" Chloe asked.

"Technically, no," Missy said. "My brothers and I were born in this country. So was my mom. But her family is from India, and so is my dad."

"So when do you wear that dress?" Kathi asked.

Missy shrugged. "This is the first time. It's been hanging in my closet ever since my grandmother gave it to me," Missy said.

Mrs. Carmichael burst out of the kitchen into the hallway. "Hello, girls," she said. "Is anyone hungry?"

"Groovy!" Kathi said like a hippie. Mrs. Carmichael gave her a perplexed look. "I mean, yes, please."

Zee led the way into the dining room. Food covered the table. There was a large plate arranged with sliced fruit. Yogurt and hummus dips and spreads sat beside a tray of sliced cucumbers, julienne carrots, asparagus, and broccoli. Breads, crackers, and rice cakes were ready to be topped with about ten different kinds of cheeses.

"Who else is coming?" Missy asked.

Zee and Chloe burst out laughing.

"What's so funny?" Missy wondered out loud.

"Mrs. Carmichael always makes a ton of food when people come over," Kathi explained.

"She can't help herself," Zee said.

"Don't you end up throwing out a lot of food?" Missy asked.

At that moment, Adam stepped into the dining room. "Hello, seventh graders," he said. He picked up a plate and started piling on fruit, crackers, and cheese.

Zee turned to Missy. "This is my brother, Adam—or as we like to call him, the human garbage disposal."

Everyone filled their plates and sat down.

"I think we should just wear these costumes for the musical," Chloe joked.

Kathi crunched on a carrot stick. "I plan to," she said seriously. "Without the giant peace sign, of course."

"And Mr. P should wear my sari for one of the scenes where he plays a woman," Missy suggested.

"Ohmylanta! You know that part where he's the nosy neighbor," Zee asked. "We should make him wear a ridiculous blond wig with a dress."

"And those beige knee-high nylon socks they sell at the drugstore!" Jen added.

"And black shoes with thick soles," Chloe suggested.

"And giant boobs," Missy put in.

"You guys!" Kathi shrieked. "Don't do that to him!" But she laughed as hard as everyone else.

"So, do you guys just want to look at the whole script and figure out the costumes for each scene?" Zee asked.

"Then Zee and I can buy or make whatever people don't already have," Kathi suggested.

"I think that for the big hip-hop dance scenes, all the girls should dress alike," Missy said. "Except Zee could have something to make her stand out as the lead."

"And Kathi, too," Jen added. "And we definitely should do the same kind of thing for the boys."

"That's pretty easy," Chloe said, "since they'll wear football uniforms."

"Except we need to figure out something special for Landon," Zee pointed out.

"Maybe he could carry a football?" Missy asked as if she was afraid to make the suggestion.

"Cool beans!" Zee said. Zee looked around the table and remembered Missy's skating party. Obviously, the other girls had thought about Zee's ideas.

Ohmylanta! Zee thought. *They weren't the problem. I was.* "To teamwork!" Zee said, holding her cup high in the air.

"And to making Mr. P look as ridiculous as possible," Chloe added.

"No way!" Kathi squealed while everyone laughed.

After dinner, the girls watched part of the first season of *Project Runway* on DVD, then went up to Zee's room to put on pajamas.

"What should we do now?" Zee asked. She wasn't tired anymore.

"Well . . . at my old school, we used to play a game

called Secrets," Missy suggested.

"How do you play that?" Jen asked.

"You have to tell the group something you've never told anyone," Missy explained.

"I'll go first," Kathi said, fingering the white fake-fur trim of her pink sleeping bag. "I'm afraid of not being perfect."

"I thought you liked being perfect!" Jen said, shocked.

"I just worry about all that stuff for my parents," Kathi told her. "They think it makes them look bad if I mess up."

"Ugh! I know. My parents want me to be a doctor like my father," Jen said.

"Don't you have to be really good in science to be a doctor?" Zee asked. Jen was Zee's lab partner, and Zee was usually the one in charge of measuring everything properly and making sure beakers didn't break.

Jen hung her head. "Yes, but I don't care about science. I want to be a writer."

"Well, I know this might sound crazy to you guys now, but I was really worried that everyone would hate me," Missy confessed.

"No way!" Kathi said in a fake shocked way. Kathi was a good actress, but Zee didn't think her performance was very convincing.

"It's probably really hard to come to a new school," Zee said.

Missy nodded, then turned to Chloe. "What's your secret, Chloe?"

Chloe bit her lip. "I don't know."

"Come on, Chloe," Zee coaxed. "Don't get shy all of a sudden. You must have a secret."

"I do," Chloe said, "but it's really someone else's secret, so I can't say anything."

"Whose?" Zee asked.

"I guess you'll have to invite 'em to your next sleepover if you want to find out," Chloe said. Then she looked at Zee. "What about you? What's your secret?"

"I guess my secret isn't really a secret since *everybody* knows I almost kissed Landon—then got grounded."

"If you ask me, you got off easy," Jen said. "My parents would ground me for *life* if I kissed a boy."

"My parents don't have to say anything," Chloe put in. "No way am I interested in kissing any boys."

"Not even Marcus?" Zee asked. How could Chloe have a crush on someone and not want to kiss him?

"No way." Chloe made a disgusted face. "I've got better things to do."

"Well, even though I never have, I would *like* to kiss a

boy," Kathi said. She turned and smiled at the other girls.

Zee had always thought Kathi and Landon had kissed when they were going out last year. *If Kathi never kissed Landon,* Zee thought, *maybe he's never kissed anyone. I'll be his first kiss, too!*

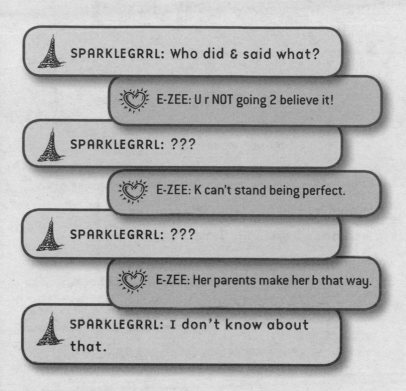

SPARKLEGRRL: Who did & said what?

E-ZEE: U r NOT going 2 believe it!

SPARKLEGRRL: ???

E-ZEE: K can't stand being perfect.

SPARKLEGRRL: ???

E-ZEE: Her parents make her b that way.

SPARKLEGRRL: I don't know about that.

E-ZEE: She told us she only acts like that b/c of them. She's being super-nice.

 SPARKLEGRRL: B careful, Z. She is PERFECTly sneaky. I wouldn't trust what she says.

 E-ZEE: Well, we r going 2 spend the rest of the day 2gether, working on costumes. We only have a week b4 the performance. She's working really hard.

 SPARKLEGRRL: Just watch out. And if she does anything, I am always here 4 u.

 E-ZEE: Good, b/c we need 2 figure out how 2 get L interested again.

Zee waited for Ally's response. Then she waited some more.

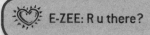 **E-ZEE: R u there?**

More waiting. Finally . . .

 SPARKLEGRRL: Sorry about that. I had 2 do something.

 E-ZEE: What?

 SPARKLEGRRL: Jacques called. I've GTG. I'm meeting him downstairs in 10 mins. I have 2 get ready. H&K.

 E-ZEE: BB4N.

Zee looked at Ally's words—*I am always here 4 u*—and everything that followed. *Is Ally really here for me? Or just for her boyfriend?* Then Zee had another horrible feeling. Could she be jealous of Ally, because everything was going really well between her and Jacques—and everything was going disastrously for Zee and Landon?

❋ 16 ❋

Conrad's Story

How to Tell If Someone Is Your BFF

1. She helps you with your problems.
2. She's always there for you.
3. She keeps your secrets.
4. She makes sure you don't totally embarrass yourself.
5. She chooses you over her boyfriend.

Hi, Diary,

I feel awful! I'm not sure if Ally and I are BFF any-more. ☹ (Look at #5 ⇑.)

The worst part is, I don't know what to do about

Landon. I need to find out what he thought of the almost-kiss. But I can't just ask. Duh! I don't know what to do. And Ally's not here for me. Could Chloe help me figure it out? Or Jasper?

Now I need a BFF to help me solve my BFF problem!

Zee

That Monday, the Beans had to stay after school to record some of the instrumentals for the final performance. They practiced the music during first period.

Usually, Mr. P was really cheerful and encouraging no matter how the class played. Not this time. He was so cranky. *Tap. Tap. Tap.* He clicked the conducting baton against his music stand. "Stop. Stop. Stop," he said, rubbing his face hard and running his fingers through his hair, so that it stuck straight up from his head.

"Let's try to get it right this time," Mr. P sighed.

Mr. P's mood was contagious and made Zee grumpy and nervous, too. She couldn't seem to play the right chords. It didn't help that Zee's mother kept giving her a smile and a thumbs-up each time they had to start over.

When the bell finally rang, Zee panicked. How would they be ready to record that afternoon?

"I feel like I'm sleepwalking," Chloe

said. She held her arms straight out in front of her and closed her eyes as she stepped forward.

"I can't believe we have to make it through the entire day," Kathi said.

"And the recording session," Jen said.

"I guess we shouldn't have stayed up so late at your house this weekend, Zee," Missy pointed out.

Zee was miserable the rest of the day. Nothing added up in math. English sounded like a foreign language. And she was antisocial in social studies.

The group met up on the auditorium stage after school. Conrad and Marcus were in charge of leading the Beans through the session.

"First, we're going to record all the songs that everyone plays," Conrad said.

Landon spoke up. "That's not a very good idea," he said. "We should start with the first song in the musical."

"That doesn't work, because we'd be spending too much time getting the different instruments set up," Conrad explained.

"I guess you don't want anyone else's opinion," Landon mumbled.

"You're doing props, but I don't remember you asking

anyone else's opinion about that," Jasper countered.

"And when I want *your* opinion, I'll let *you* know," Landon said.

"I'm just saying that we each have our job," Jasper explained.

"Well, your job is assistant director," Landon added. "You're not in charge of music—or me!"

The boys were having the same argument that the girls had had! Zee thought she could help. "Actually," Zee cut in, "I thought it was really great when the other girls made suggestions about costumes."

But the boys didn't want Zee's help.

Conrad said, "We don't have enough time for that." Jasper glared at Zee. And Landon looked away.

"Let's start recording the songs that everyone plays in and if it seems like it's not working, we can switch the order," Marcus said diplomatically.

"Marcus is right!" Chloe said. "It can't hurt to try it Conrad's way."

"I really don't think Conrad needs you to defend him," Jen said.

"Who asked you?" Chloe snapped back.

"All of this fighting isn't very helpful," Missy put in.

The next instant, everyone was arguing—except Kathi,

who sat down on the edge of the stage. It was hard to hear what anyone was saying. Mrs. Carmichael swooped in. "Shhh!" she hushed the group.

"Let's calm down, everyone," Mr. P added.

Gradually, shouts turned to murmurs—until everyone was quiet enough to hear Conrad's phone ring. "Hello, Obachan," he said quietly, stepping to the side of the stage. "Yes, I'll be home in time for dinner." He said good-bye and hung up.

"Was that your mother?" Zee asked when Conrad returned to the group.

Conrad looked at Marcus. "Umm . . . no," Conrad said. "It was my grandmother. She lives with me and my dad— ever since my mom got sick."

"She takes care of your mom?" Jen asked.

"She takes care of me—and Dad," Conrad explained seriously. "My mom died a couple of months ago. She had cancer."

No one knew what to say. Zee felt terrible and wasn't even sure where to look. Then Landon stepped forward and broke the awkward silence. "That's so cool that you live with your grandmother," he said. "My grandparents are awesome! I wish I could see them every day, but they live halfway across the country."

"Yeah, Obachan's fun, but she can be pretty overprotective," Conrad said.

Zee looked over at her mother. "I know what you mean," she said, just above a whisper. Mrs. Carmichael crossed her arms, shook her head, and pursed her lips, trying to hold back a smile.

The Beans burst out laughing and everyone took a chair. Just a few days ago, Zee never would have guessed that her troubles with her mother would actually be what kept the group together.

"You guys have never sounded better!" Mr. P applauded when the recording session was over. His hair no longer stuck straight up, and he wore a huge smile. "Let's give Conrad and Marcus a hand for leading us."

Whistling and cheering loudly, Landon was the first to give the guys a standing ovation. Everyone else followed.

"And let's hear it for the rest of the Beans, who played so well," Mr. P went on.

The applause got louder as Marcus and Conrad joined in.

"I'm going to put these paints back in the art room," Zee's mother told her when the noise faded. "Meet me in the lobby when you're packed up and ready to go."

"Okay, Mom," Zee agreed. She raced to put away

her instrument. She had finally figured out a plan to fix things between Landon and her. It was time to put it in motion.

Zee walked over to where Landon and Conrad were talking. Landon was still sitting behind his drum kit.

"You and your dad should come sailing with my family on our boat sometime," Zee overheard Landon saying. "Your grandmother can come, too."

"She'd like that! She'd want to be captain, though, since she's used to being in charge." Conrad smiled, then the smile disappeared as he continued, "I thought you hated me."

"I probably was kind of being a jerk," Landon said. "Sorry about that."

"We're cool now," Conrad said, holding his fist out for Landon to pound.

As Conrad walked away, Zee moved closer to Landon. "Your drum solo was so great," Zee told him, smiling.

But Landon didn't look up as he reached for his drumsticks and stood. "Uh . . . I gotta go catch up with Marcus and Conrad," he said, hurrying off.

What's going on? Zee wondered. Her mother wasn't even around. And now there was no doubt in Zee's mind—Landon wished she didn't exist. *How can we perform together as Lily and Dylan if Landon won't even look at me?*

Hi, Diary,

I think the musical is ruined. Landon doesn't want to come near me. Why does he hate me? Three possibilities ⇓

1. He's embarrassed about the "kind of" kiss.
2. He's afraid of my mother.
3. He did give me that Friends' Day card, and now he wishes he didn't.

What can I do to get him to talk to me again? Is our crush doomed—like Lily and Dylan's? ☹

Zee

17

Friends

  E-ZEE: R u out there?

  SPARKLEGRRL is offline

Just when Zee needed her best friend most, Ally was around less and less.

Zee texted Chloe.

>Can u talk?
>Not now. @ school w J. Working in garden.

Chloe and Jasper were too busy for her. *It doesn't matter,*

Zee thought. Maybe she'd never be able to figure out Landon, but the show must go on. She was going over to Kathi's house to put the final touches on costumes.

Zee pushed her bicycle out of her garage and strapped on her helmet, which she had painted with a giant red Z, and rode over to Kathi's house.

Kathi and Zee sat in the gazebo next to the pool in the Barneys' backyard. Kathi beaded a pair of hoop earrings she would wear in the big dance scene. "I feel like a pioneer making my own stuff," she complained.

"I don't think the pioneers wore bikinis," Zee said jokingly as she carefully stitched gold thread onto the pocket of Missy's costume.

"No wonder they're not around anymore. Who could survive without bikinis? Anyway," Kathi continued, "I'm talking about all of this crafty stuff. I mean, there's a reason they invented designer boutiques."

"I think it's fun," Zee said. "Plus, we didn't really have enough money for a trip to Rodeo Drive."

"At least this will all be over soon," Kathi said. "The musical is in two days."

Two days. Zee's stomach sank. "I'm not sure I'm ready,"

she told Kathi.

"Are you kidding? You know all your lines—and your songs," Kathi pointed out.

"It's not that." Zee stopped sewing. "It's just . . ." She hesitated.

"What?" Kathi asked, her voice concerned. "I won't tell anyone."

Ally's words rang in Zee's head. *I wouldn't trust what she says.* But Ally wasn't there for Zee. Kathi was.

"Everything is so messed up with Landon," Zee said. "I mean, he only rehearses with me when he *has* to. And now he won't even look at me."

"What's going on?"

"I think the kiss—I mean, the almost-kiss—messed up our friendship. Or whatever it is." Zee hung her head. "It'll be all my fault if the musical is ruined."

"*Your* fault?" Kathi said. "You've worked harder than anyone."

Did Kathi just pay me a compliment? Zee considered poking herself with the needle she was holding to make sure she wasn't dreaming.

"Except me," Kathi continued.

Okay. I'm awake, Zee told herself. "What should I do?" she asked.

"Just do your best in the musical," Kathi suggested. "You can't do anything about Landon. He's always been a little immature. Most of the time, it doesn't matter since he's so cool and cute. But sometimes it makes it hard to know what's going on with him. Besides, he might just be scared of his first kiss."

"Do you really think so?" Zee asked, surprised. She hadn't even considered that boys think about kissing, too—and that Landon might have been just as nervous about the near-kiss as she was.

Kathi slipped the finished hoops through her ears and shook her head to show off her work. "Older men are so different," she said dreamily.

"Ohmylanta!" Zee shouted. "Mr. P is a teacher!"

"I know he doesn't like me like *that*," Kathi said, shrugging. "But it's still more fun to have a crush on an older guy. It's so much less complicated."

"If you say so." Zee rolled her eyes as both girls began laughing uncontrollably.

 SPARKLEGRRL: I kissed him!

There Ally was. Finally. And she'd actually kissed Jacques!

 E-ZEE: How was it?

 SPARKLEGRRL: Not what I expected.

 E-ZEE: 411

 SPARKLEGRRL: His lips were dry. And he mostly missed mine.

 E-ZEE: U will have 2 keep practicing.

 SPARKLEGRRL: LOL!!!

 E-ZEE: So how can I get L 2 kiss me? Or @ least stop being all weird.

 SPARKLEGRRL: Mayb u r trying 2 hard.

 E-ZEE: ???

 SPARKLEGRRL: U haven't even gone out. That comes 1st.

At that point, Zee couldn't imagine going out with Landon since they were barely talking. But Ally was right. Zee was rushing everything. Landon wasn't ready. And Zee had let the near-kiss mess up everything with her friends and the musical.

Kathi had a point, too. The *crush* was the fun part. For now, a crush was enough. Then Zee realized— "Ohmylanta!"—her parents had been right all along.

Zee went downstairs where her parents were practicing for their salsa dance classes. They looked like they were having a great time, with every step in sync. Zee hoped she looked that good dancing in the musical.

"Mom? Dad?" Zee got their attention from the bottom of the stairway.

"What is it, Zee?" her dad asked.

"I just wanted to apologize for acting so crazy these past few weeks," Zee continued.

"Oh?" Mrs. Carmichael said in a way that meant she was eager to hear more.

"I think I got a little carried away," Zee told them.

"With the musical?" Mr. Carmichael asked.

Zee nodded, then hung her head. "And Landon. He's barely even talking to me now."

"That's not good." Zee's mom looked surprised.

"What's going on?"

"I'm not exactly sure. But I'd like to call him—if it's okay with you. I need to fix this before the performance."

Zee's parents looked at each other and gave a little nod. "That would be fine," her father said.

Zee searched her contact list and called Landon quickly so she wouldn't chicken out.

"Hello?" Landon answered, sounding suspicious.

"It's Zee."

"Uh-huh?"

"I'm just calling to make sure we're cool," Zee began.

"Umm . . ."

"I mean, I really want to be friends—and costars. But it seems like you don't want to be my friend, ever since"—Zee stopped, trying to find the right words—"we went skating."

"Yeah . . . ," Landon said, as though he was really considering what Zee had said. "It has been kind of weird. You just want to be friends?"

"Sure," Zee said. "*Aren't* we friends?"

"Yeah, we're friends."

"Cool beans!" Zee said, relieved. "Do you think we should go over some lines together before the show?"

"Yeah, let's meet at school an hour before the show and practice."

"Fantabsome! I'll be there!"

Zee turned on her computer. She had to tell her best friend what had happened.

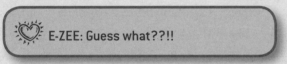

E-ZEE: Guess what??!!

But the only response Zee got was a message that Ally was offline. Zee told her all about it in an email instead.

A,
What would I do w/o u? I would have made a total
fool of myself, that's what. Landon & I r cool now.
IM me 4 the details ASAP! U r the best!
<333,
Z

18

No-show Time

As soon as Zee woke up Sunday morning, she checked her email. Still nothing from Ally! It had been two days since Zee had emailed her. Zee couldn't imagine why Ally hadn't written her back. Was she too busy with Jacques?

Hi, Diary,

Where's Ally? I really need her. Even though Landon and I worked things out, I'm still scared about the performance. What if I freeze up and forget my lines? Or one of the costumes malfunctions? I thought I was ready, but now I'm not sure.

There are a million things that could go wrong!

Mostly, it just seems like Ally doesn't care. I miss my best friend.

Zee

*　*　*

The Beans had been practicing all morning. For the first half hour of the day, the sound equipment screeched and squealed—until Marcus's brother, Samuel, moved a few cables and pushed some buttons. Missy's E-string broke in the middle of her solo, so she had to stop and put on a new one. Then a piece of the set got stuck and wouldn't budge. That time, Mrs. Carmichael was there to coax it back on track.

Finally, they were rehearsing the last ensemble number.

The boys moved low across the stage like football players avoiding their opponents.

"Watch out!" the football players shouted at Landon in song. *"She's just a dancer!"*

Zee and the girls were in the middle of a hip-hop dance, bending and waving their arms. *"No way!"* the girls responded to the boys in a musical shouting match. *"He's not the answer!"*

Zee threw her arms up as part of the dance. *Riiiippp.* The seam in the side of her shirt tore. Zee rushed offstage, holding the torn seam together with her hands.

"Take a break, everyone!" Jasper shouted in a very un-Jasperlike way. "We'll pick it up there when Zee is ready."

Mrs. Carmichael rushed over with a needle and thread.

"Lift up your arm," she said, carefully pushing the needle back and forth without poking Zee. "There! Good as new."

"You're the best, Mom!" Zee said, giving her a kiss on the cheek. "I'm so glad you were here to help out."

"Oh?" Mrs. Carmichael said, grinning slightly. "I thought you thought I was overprotective."

"Who me?" Zee said innocently. "What gave you that idea?"

"It doesn't really matter now, does it?" Zee's mom responded. "You'd better get back onstage or there won't be a show tonight!"

"From the top of the scene!" Jasper boomed. This time they made it to the end without a mishap. When they finished, Zee realized that she was so worried about the musical, she hadn't even thought about Landon once.

Mr. P ran his fingers through his hair, which was flipping and flopping every which way. "Come on over here for a few quick announcements," he said, waving them over in his direction. The cast sat down in the first row of auditorium seats.

The teacher shoved his hands in the front pockets of his blue jeans and leaned against the stage. "Thanks for working so hard, everyone! I think we got all the glitches out, and the world is ready to meet the Beans."

"Yay!" the band shouted. Their energy could have lit up the entire stage.

"Tonight I'd like you to get your costumes on—boys in the main drama room and girls in the music room—then meet me backstage thirty minutes before showtime."

While Mr. P was speaking, Kathi turned to whisper in Zee's ear. "I forgot to tell you one thing about the costu—"

"Kathi, please let me finish what I have to say," Mr. P interrupted her. "Then you can talk all you want."

Kathi's mouth dropped open. She tried to speak, but nothing came out. As Kathi stared down at her hands, Zee wondered, *Is she going to cry?*

Mr. P finished his speech by telling everyone to "break a leg!" and everyone started talking. But before Zee could make sure Kathi was okay, Kathi flung her bag over her shoulder and rushed out of the auditorium.

"What's the matter with her?" Jasper asked.

"I think Mr. P embarrassed her," Zee said.

"Not hardly," Chloe said, shocked. "She never gets embarrassed. She usually does the embarrassing."

"I don't know," Zee said, thinking back on all of the new things she'd learned about Kathi over the past few weeks. "She might not be who we thought."

That evening, Zee's mother dropped her at the Brookdale Academy auditorium entrance an hour before the show. To save time, Zee had put on her costume and makeup at home.

"Daddy, Adam, and I will be back in time for the show," Mrs. Carmichael told Zee.

"Get here early so you can get a good seat," Zee said.

"Of course we will!" Mrs. Carmichael said. "Your dad and I are very proud of you." Her eyes started to glisten from tears.

"Please don't make me cry," Zee said. "I spent an hour on my makeup, and I don't want to have to redo it." She hopped onto the sidewalk and blew her mother a kiss. "I love you."

Zee walked through the auditorium and stopped to look at the amazing set that Chloe and Missy had made for the first scene—the hip-hop dance studio, complete with floor-to-ceiling mirrors and a fake window that looked out onto a block of brick Los Angeles row houses. She turned to the empty seats and pictured them filled with the Beans' families and friends.

Then Zee pushed open one of the doors that led to the music hall. A sign that read, SHHHH! PLEASE TURN OFF ALL CELL PHONES AND MOBILE DEVICES hung next to it.

"Oops!" Zee said, pulling out her Sidekick and turning it off. *That would be embarrassing.* Then, with preshow butterflies in her stomach, Zee looked for her costar.

"That was really great!" Landon told Zee after they'd finished running through their first duet. "I just hope I don't get nervous in front of all those people and mess it up."

"Why don't we come up with a way to help each other calm down if either of us starts to freak out?" Zee suggested.

"Like what?"

"I don't know." Zee thought. "How about a handshake? Ally and I used to do one. We'd high-five, then low-five, then shake, and bump right shoulders together."

"Uh . . . that sounds pretty complicated," Landon told her.

"It's not. I'll show you," Zee said. "High five. Low five." Landon caught on easily. "Shake." Landon took her hand. "And bump right shoulders." They leaned toward each other.

"That's where you guys are hiding!" Kathi said before

Zee even realized anyone else had come into the hallway.

Zee dropped Landon's hand. "We weren't hiding!" she answered immediately. Even though it was true, she felt as though she'd been caught doing something wrong.

"Whatev." Kathi shrugged. "Mr. P wants you guys on-stage."

Landon and Zee started to move. Kathi put her hand on Zee's shoulder. "Wait a sec, Zee," she said. "There's one scene I want to talk to you about real quick—best friend to best friend."

"Oh, okay," Zee said. "But we should make it fast."

"I'll let Mr. P know you guys are coming," Landon said, rushing off toward the stage door.

Kathi watched Landon disappear, then turned to Zee. "I thought you weren't going to kiss him," Kathi hissed accusatorily.

"What . . . huh . . . I . . ." Zee said, looking around frantically. "That?" She giggled nervously. "That was—"

Before Zee could say more, Kathi pushed her. She fell backward—right into an open practice room.

"Hey!" Zee shouted, hurrying to stand. *Slam!* Kathi shut the door before she could get out. Zee turned the handle, but it wouldn't budge. *Kathi must have jammed it with something,* Zee thought. She was stuck inside.

Zee pounded on the door. "Let me out!" She had to yell at the top of her lungs, because the room was soundproof.

"Not until you learn to keep your hands off Landon!" Kathi shouted back.

"Ohmylanta," Zee groaned to herself. Then, she yelled to Kathi, "You said you were only crushing on older guys."

"As if! I've moved on."

"Landon and I are just friends," Zee called out. But Kathi didn't say anything. "Kathi?" Zee raised her voice a little. "Kathi!" And louder. "Kaaaaathiiiii!"

Kathi was gone! And Zee was still locked in the room! *Don't panic*, Zee told herself, taking out her Sidekick. She texted Chloe and Jasper.

>Help! Im trapped n a practice rm!

Then she waited. For nothing.

Zee tried again—to Landon. No answer. She couldn't give up. She had to get out. Next she sent the message to

Missy, Conrad, and Marcus. *Of course*, Zee realized. *No one is getting my texts because they all turned off their cell phones for the show.*

The cast had, but maybe Zee's family hadn't. She quickly sent her plea to her mother, father, and Adam, then stared at the screen. No response.

"Heeeellllllp!" Zee screamed and pounded on the door. *It's no use*, she thought, sliding down the wall until she was sitting on the floor. *No one can hear me.*

Zee would miss the Beans' debut. Would she be stuck in the room all night? She was desperate. Normally, Zee wasn't allowed to text Ally because it was too expensive, but Zee did the only thing she could do. She texted her anyway. She had no one else to talk to—and it was going to be a long night.

>U were right! K tricked me again! Thx 2
her, I am going 2 miss the show. I am stuck
in a practice rm. WB.

Zee didn't actually expect Ally to respond. But this time she had a good excuse—her friend was sound asleep on another continent.

Then Zee curled up into a ball and sobbed.

19

The Show Must Go On

The practice room door flew open. Zee looked up from the floor. Ally towered over her in the doorway. *Ally?* Were the tears clouding Zee's eyes?

Ally reached out her hand. "Get up!"

Still in shock, Zee did. "What are you doing here?" she asked.

"I don't have time to explain," Ally said. "You need to get onstage! It's three minutes to showtime!"

"But—"

"I'll explain later," Ally told her. "Come on! You're the star of a musical."

"Are you really here, or is this just a dream?" Zee asked, obediently following Ally down the hall and onto the stage.

All of the band members were crowded around Mr. P.

"I've got to get over there and tell Mr. P what happened," Zee said.

Ally grabbed Zee's arm. "Wait!" she said, reaching into her purse. "I have to fix your makeup. After all that crying, you look like you've been in a prizefight." She got out a tissue and started wiping Zee's face. Then she pulled out a tube of mascara.

"No way!" Zee said. "You have mascara in your purse? Do you get to wear makeup?"

"Yes!" Ally said. "That's one of a zillion things we have to talk about. Now hold still while I put it on."

"I don't know where Zee is," Kathi told the teacher while Ally applied Zee's makeup. "She seemed really scared when I went to get her. Maybe she got stage fright."

Mr. P looked terrified. "Missy," he said, "you'll have to go on as Lily."

"But Zee has the costume," Missy protested.

Mr. P wiped sweat from his forehead. "Yours will be

fine," Mr. P said. "Places, everyone! It's showtime."

The students scattered to get into position behind the closed curtain.

"Mr. P!" Zee shouted across the stage, then raced to her teacher's side.

"There you are! What happened?" Mr. P asked. His face looked more relieved than angry.

Zee looked at Kathi. Panicked, Kathi said, "Zee, what are—?"

"Sorry," Zee said to Mr. P, interrupting Kathi. "I'm such a klutz. I locked myself in a practice room." As awful as Kathi was, Zee wouldn't stoop to her level by telling on her. She wasn't interested in causing trouble.

"Am I glad you're here!" Missy said, giving Zee a hug. "I could never play Lily like you do. Break a leg!"

"I will!" Zee said. She decided not to mention whose leg she'd like to break.

The show was fantabsome. Everyone was in step with the choreography and in tune with the singing. Mr. Vasi filmed the entire performance, so the Beans could watch it over and over again.

After getting locked in the practice room, Zee figured she deserved an award for playing Kathi's best friend.

Conrad stole the show with his crazy sense of humor. Chloe and Marcus looked like they were having a great time. Jasper showed that he wasn't the shy kid everyone thought he was. And Missy's violin solo was so amazing it practically stopped the whole show.

And Landon? He was a great actor as well as the most gorgeous boy at Brookdale. And he and Zee had their chemistry back—even if it was just pretend.

20

Party Girl

"You're not mad that Kathi locked you in that room?" Ally asked Zee at the cast party after the performance.

"I would have been surprised if she *hadn't* done something like that," Zee said, laughing.

Conrad's father started out deejaying the party, but Conrad took over. Kathi hogged Landon on the dance floor, while Marcus, Missy, and Jen danced nearby, although Jen did not look happy about sharing Marcus.

"Okay," Chloe said to Ally. "Remind me again how you got here without Zee knowing about it."

"Ginny arranged it," Ally said.

"Ginny?" Chloe looked shocked. "You call Zee's mom by her first name?"

"Yeah," Zee said. "I guess because Ally's known my mom forever."

Ally shrugged. "Anyway, I'm going to stay with Zee's family while my parents are traveling for two weeks for work."

Zee gave Ally a playful shove. "And they kept it a secret from me. So when I didn't get an IM or email for two days, I thought Ally was ignoring me." Then Zee leaned in to whisper, "The whole time Mom was trying to keep me and Landon apart, she was trying to get me and Ally together."

"Uh . . . no whispering please," Jasper said, joining the group.

"Oh, my gosh!" Chloe suddenly burst out laughing. "Did you see the look on Ms. Merriweather's face in the third scene? It was just like when the handle fell off the wheelbarrow during the garden workday."

Zee, Chloe, and Jasper cracked up at the memory.

"I don't get it," Ally said. "What happened?"

Chloe waved her hand in the air. "It's too complicated to explain."

"What about when Missy hit that really high note?" Zee said. "I thought Conrad was going to do what he did at the ISC."

"That was hilarious!" Chloe added.

"What was it?" Ally asked.

"Well, Missy was skating, and Conrad came up behind her. . . ." Zee trailed off. "I think you had to be there."

"Oh," Ally said, hanging her head.

Zee felt bad. Ally had been at Brookdale Academy longer than Chloe or Jasper, yet she seemed like an outsider. "Hey, Jasper. Ally just went to London," Zee said, hoping to save her friend.

"Really?" Jasper said. "Did you have tea with the queen?" As Ally cracked up, a smile spread across Jasper's face.

Ally told Jasper all about where she stayed, ate, and visited.

"I've always wanted to go to the Tower of London," Zee put in.

Ally scrunched up her nose. "That's kind of touristy. I went to a lot of places no one's ever heard of"—she looked at Jasper—"except the natives."

"I guess I'm not a very sophisticated traveler," Zee mumbled.

"I think I'd like to freshen up my punch," Jasper said. "Your cup looks empty, Ally. Would you like some more?"

"Yes, please," Ally said, handing him her cup.

As Jasper walked to the refreshment table, Ally excitedly turned to Zee. "Does he like anyone?"

What was with everyone liking Jasper! A weird feeling wrapped around Zee's heart. Just as she was about to say, "No," Jasper's eyes reached across the room—looking right past Ally at Zee. His mouth stretched into a wide smile before he picked up the clear plastic ladle and began pouring out the red punch.

Zee smiled back. As her stomach flipped, then flopped, she had a funny feeling she finally knew who had sent her the mysterious Friends' Day card.

* * *

Hi, Diary,

I think Jasper is my secret admirer. But I kind of like not knowing for sure. I wasted so much time caring about crushes, I almost messed up everything with Landon. I don't want to ruin my friendship with Jasper. Besides, that's all the card said—"a great friend." I can't believe I freaked out about a nice card from a good friend. No wonder he couldn't tell me he wrote it. I way overreacted.

Zee flipped back through her diary and looked at the list of names she had made on Friends' Day. Zee knew just what to add:

Who Could My Secret Admirer Be?		
Suspect	Motive	Degree of Suspicion
Jasper ☺	We're friends!	6 (No biggie!)

Online Glossary

&	and
@	at
<3 (sideways heart)	= love (<33 = extra love)
=	equal
1	one
1st	first
2	to; two; too
2day	today
2-faced	two-faced
2gether	together
2morrow	tomorrow
2nite	tonight
4	for
411	information
4get	forget
4give	forgive
4gotten	forgotten

ASAP	as soon as possible
b	be
b/c	because
b/f	boyfriend
b4	before
BB4N	bye-bye for now
BFF	best friends forever
bz	busy
c	see
CA	California
cld	could
every1	everyone
g/f	girlfriend
gr8	great
GTG	gotta go
GTR	gotta run
H&K	hugs and kisses
LOL	laughing out loud
LYLAS	love you like a sister
mayb	maybe
mins	minutes
MUSM	miss you so much
NK	no kidding
no1	no one

NP	no problem
nt	not
OMG	oh, my God
OMGYG2BK	oh, my God, you've got to be kidding
pic	picture
pls	please
r	are
rm	room
thm	them
thx	thanks
TTFN	ta-ta for now
u	you
u'll	you'll
ur	your; you're
urs	yours
w	with
w/o	without
WB	write back
WFM	works for me
ws	was
y	why

Acknowledgments

Well, here we go again! I must first say a big thank-you to Mackenzie's godmothers, Catherine Onder and Tara Weikum. Special thanks to my entire HarperCollins team: Susan Katz, Elise Howard, Kate Jackson, Diane Naughton, Cristina Gilbert, and Laura Kaplan. You've made this experience such a pleasure.

To my A-Team: Kate Lee, words can't express the gratitude I have for all the work you've done on my behalf. It's such a pleasure to work with you. Andre Des Rochers, thank you for always making sure I'm heard—even when I'm not there. And, of course, a special thank-you goes out to my lifetime quarterback Marissa Nance, who always makes sure I'm surrounded by the best. Thank you for caring.

To my family: Mom, Dad, Adrianne, Erica, Marcus, Lisa, and William—thank you all for being there for me and supporting me through this process. I couldn't do it without you!

To my girls: Michelle Moragne, Nurys Iza, Monica Rush, Jackie Fucini, Suny Rodriguez, Karen Otero, Kimberly Lyons, Tia Williams, Stephanie Smith, Melissa Nasir, and my dearest friend, Tina Pittaoulis—thank you all for keeping me sane and making sure I'm taken care of every day. You're the smartest, most loving, most beautiful women I know! Love you all!

To Ross Martin, Dave Knox, and Marc Feuerstein: Thanks for all your support and great advice. It means a lot.

Finally, to my children from another mother: Azairea, Zoey, Daishawn, and RJ—thanks for listening to my stories and giving me great advice. Dayna and Rodney, thank you for letting me borrow your children. ;-)

Read on for a sneak peek at
Mackenzie's next adventure!

"It'll be great to get some fresh air and commune with na-ture, huh, guys?" Adam said, looking right at Zee. He sucked in deeply as if he were standing on the top of Brookdale Mountain.

Zee had lived long enough with her seventeen-year-old brother to know she was being taunted. "How about you commune with nature, and I'll stay home in my comfort-able bed?"

"Uh . . . how about no," Adam countered. "I already went on the Brookdale Mountain field trip when I was in seventh grade. Your turn."

"We'll just be gone until Friday, Zee," Chloe reminded her.

"That's five whole days," Adam repeated. "It should give me enough time to convert the twins' bedroom into a sau-na." He called Ally and Zee "the twins" because before Ally moved, they were practically inseparable. Sometimes they even dressed alike. That day Zee and Ally both had on blue jeans with tiny flowers they'd embroidered at the bottom. They topped off their outfits with matching long-sleeved T-shirts.

"Very funny," Zee said sarcastically to Adam, even though everyone really was laughing. "If even one piece of paper is out of place . . . ," she threatened.

"And how would you be able to tell?" Adam asked.

Zee paused. Her room was usually a disorganized mess.

Suddenly, a shout rang across the parking lot. "Everyone, it's time to board the bus!" Ms. Merriweather, Brookdale Academy's seventh-grade science teacher was gathering students together.

Zee looked at her friends. "Let's go!" Maybe the science trip wouldn't be so bad. After all, she'd be missing a week of school and hanging out with her best friends in the world.

Zee, Ally, Jasper, and Chloe placed their luggage on the heap with the rest of the seventh graders' bags. As they walked toward the bus steps, they were joined by the rest of the boys in the fifth-period science class—Marcus Montgomery, Conrad Mitori, and Landon Beck—*the* cutest boy at Brookdale Academy.

All the boys got on the bus, but Adam grabbed Zee's shoulder. "Wait!" he said.

"What?" Zee asked. Ally and Chloe turned toward him, too.

"Watch out for the Mountain Man," Adam warned.

"Oh, please," Ally said, snorting.

When Adam's serious expression didn't change, Zee said, "The Mountain Man?"

"He lives on Brookdale Mountain. . . ." Adam stopped and shook his head. "Never mind. Maybe he won't bother you."

"Probably not," Ally said, "since he doesn't exist."

"Who's the Mountain Man?" Chloe asked.

Adam wore a faraway expression. "I remember my seventh-grade field trip like it was yesterday." He turned to look at the crowd around him. By now, the rest of Zee's science class, Kathi Barney, Jen Calverez, and Missy Vasi, had gathered to listen.

"What happened?" Zee asked.

"Someone—or should I say, some*thing*—lived on the mountain."

"Wasn't he human?" Chloe wondered.

"Well," Adam began, "he walked upright and wore human clothes, but he had hair all over his body."

"Ewww!" Kathi exclaimed. "Even on his back?"

Adam nodded. "Everywhere. Legend has it that he can't speak, so he grunts. There's only one phrase he says."

"What?" Chloe whispered, mesmerized.

"I . . . want . . . my . . . leg . . . back."

"He's missing a leg? How does he walk?" Ally asked suspiciously.

"He uses a crutch," Adam answered immediately.

As Zee's stomach twisted with fear, she wished she could be more like Ally. Zee was already nervous about being away from her parents for five days, and Adam was not helping.

"He limps down from the mountain every year during the field trip," Adam continued.

"Really?" Kathi asked. "I've never heard that, and I know a lot of eighth graders—one in particular."

Zee knew Kathi wanted everyone to ask what she meant by "one in particular," but Adam barreled ahead. "Even if no one actually sees him," he told her, "there's usually evidence that he's been near the cabins."

Marcus stuck his face through the open bus window above their heads. "Hey!" he shouted at the girls. "It's time to go!"